THE OCEAN BETWEEN US
TRINITY LAKES ROMANCE
BOOK TWO

MEREDITH RESCE

THE OCEAN BETWEEN US

TRINITY LAKES ROMANCE
BOOK TWO

MEREDITH RESCE

Golden Grain Publishing

The Ocean Between Us
Book 2 Trinity Lakes Romance series
Copyright © 2023 by Meredith Resce
The National Library of Australia Cataloguing-in-Publication Information:

A catalogue record for this
work is available from the
National Library of Australia

978-0-6489537-7-7 — eBook
978-0-6489537-8-4 — Paperback

Cover Art by Melissa Dalley

❀ Created with Vellum

CHAPTER ONE

Thank goodness the day was over. Caleb Kennedy yawned. It had been like that all day—Caleb yawning. He hadn't slept well following last night's momentous occasion. He was engaged. Engaged! Not exactly how he'd thought his engagement would happen. Somehow, he'd imagined it would have been more … what? More romantic? He'd expected he would have felt something like fireworks shooting multi-colored sparks across his universe. Something like the way he'd felt on the night of his high school formal. That was a lifetime ago and a world away. He'd finished his high schooling in Australia and wound up the year with a formal. Not a prom like they did here in Trinity Lakes, USA. No prom king and queen or arriving in a limo, but something in the way of dressing up and going out, dancing and food. And kissing Alanah at the finish. That hadn't been just sparks. That had been like a Chinese New Year.

Whoa. Why was he thinking about Alanah Walker after all this time? Sure, his twin sister, Sasha, had mentioned her best friend would be coming to Trinity Lakes for Sasha's wedding, but that was later in the year. Crazy that memories of Alanah had popped up when he was thinking about mind-blowing chemistry. Now *there* was romance and passion. That was what he'd expected when he'd finally agreed to marry Kyla. Is that why he'd put it off for so long and why he hadn't even looked at rings when he asked the question?

Hold on. How inappropriate was that line of thought? Sure, it was one of the best memories of his life ... but at a time when he should have been thinking of nothing but Kyla? His brand-new fiancée. The two memories met like opposing weather systems, and a drop in pressure hit. That wasn't good.

Caleb grabbed his water bottle and took a mouthful. He needed to get focused. Why wasn't he more stoked about what had happened last night? A thought tickled the edge of his mind. He should push the thought away, but it kept hassling him. Kyla had been the one who'd pushed him to finally propose. She'd been dropping hints like Hansel and Gretel dropped bread-crumbs. Every birthday, every Valentine's, every Christmas, every Independence Day—any day that marked some sort of celebration seemed a likely day for a proposal in Kyla's mind. He'd pretended he hadn't understood her obvious clues, but that game had worn thin, and it had been time to take the plunge. It had been a lackluster performance, if he was honest. No thought had gone into it. Why?

Kyla didn't seem to have noticed. She'd been thrilled and threw her arms around his neck and kissed him. Her exuberance seemed to mask his lack of animation. Was that a problem? Would they have a good marriage? He and Kyla shared the same faith and she worked with him in the local church youth group. She was musical, like him. The best part? She was American, and her family lived in Trinity Lakes.

That was where things had fallen apart with Alanah. She was Australian—so Aussie it was impossible to separate her from her country or her family. When Mom and Dad had decided to return to Trinity Lakes to look after Gran and Gramps, his passion couldn't bridge the geographical distance between them. Australia was called Down Under for good reason. Literally the other side of the world. Stop thinking about Alanah!

Caleb turned the "closed" sign around on the shop door. His final music student had left, and there were no more customers. Now to get home and crash on the couch. He got in the truck and backed out onto the street, but he hadn't gone fifty yards before his phone rang. Mom's name came up on the screen.

"Hey, Mom. What's up?"

"Sasha's had an accident."

"What?" Caleb braked without thinking and a car nearly rammed him from behind. "What?" He recovered from his reflexive action and accelerated again. "What happened?"

"Not sure. I just got a call from the hospital in Walla Walla."

"Walla Walla?" A stab of fear hit hard. It must be serious if they couldn't use the local hospital.

"They rushed her there for emergency surgery." Mom sounded upset, which added to Caleb's concern. "Can you go straight there?"

Caleb did a U-turn. Walla Walla was a good forty-five minutes from Trinity Lakes, the other direction from home. "Are you driving over as well?"

"I'll wait for Dad. He's finishing with the staff meeting at school."

"How serious is it? Do you want me to pick you up on the way past?"

"Yes, please pick me up. I don't know how serious it is, but if they couldn't treat her at the Trinity Lakes hospital ..." Mom stalled, obviously emotional. He felt it too. Being taken to Walla Walla was not good news. "They said something about her being in surgery. I'd prefer to get there sooner than later."

Caleb took a right turn to go past Trinity Lakes High School. Mom was walking down the front steps as he pulled into the parking lot.

"Thanks, Caleb." She latched her seatbelt as Caleb set off again.

"Who called you?" Caleb asked.

"The hospital."

"Did they tell you what happened?"

She shook her head. Caleb cast a glance in her direction. Her eyes were bright with tears.

"I'm sure she's gonna be okay." Caleb put his hand on Mom's arm. He hoped Sasha would be okay. She was as close to him as anyone in the family, being his twin.

"She was working at the campgrounds today. She'd volunteered to help with some repairs on the cabins."

"Do you have the campground's number? The supervisor?"

Mom swiped her phone open and scrolled. She punched the screen and put the phone to her ear.

"Hi, Stuart. This is Marianne Kennedy from the high school ... Yes, Sasha is my daughter ... Oh. I see. How bad was it?"

"What happened?" Caleb couldn't wait for her to finish to get the answer. This was Sasha. Mom held up her hand.

"Right. Yes, we're on the way to the hospital in Walla Walla now ... Okay. Thank you."

"What happened?" Caleb asked again.

"She was cleaning pine needles out of the gutters in preparation for fire season."

"She fell off a roof?"

"That was the result. Apparently, a gust of wind blew a branch from a nearby tree, and she sidestepped it to avoid being knocked over."

"But fell over anyway?"

"And tumbled off the roof onto the ground."

The conversation fell silent as the miles passed beneath them on the way to the neighboring community. Walla Walla was a much larger town than Trinity Lakes, with more amenities, like a large hospital equipped for major surgery. Caleb's gut twisted with worry again at the thought.

His anxiety rose as they arrived, parked his vehicle, and asked at the reception desk where they would find Sasha. *Please, Lord, let her be all right.*

"It will be another half hour before she's out of recovery." Mom made a beeline for the elevators. Caleb followed, still worried for his sister's welfare.

When they came to the waiting area outside the operating room, they were met by a doctor in scrubs.

"Are you family of Sasha Kennedy?"

"Mother, brother." Mom pointed to herself and him.

"Sasha's fine. She's come through the surgery with no issues."

"What happened? We've only heard she fell from a roof."

"She's broken her leg in two places. A bad break, and we've had to plate the bone in one place. She'll recover and be back to normal after physical therapy."

"Can we see her?" Mom asked.

"She's in recovery now, and probably emerging from the anesthetic already. She won't be alert for a little while yet, but you can sit with her."

The doctor turned and indicated they should follow.

Caleb wasn't a fan of hospitals, and even less so when he was waiting on the well-being of someone close to him.

There she was, her leg elevated and bandaged, and she was awake.

"Idiot," Caleb said, trying to hide his fear. He came beside her and took her hand.

"Thanks." She still sounded groggy.

"I can't believe you fell off a roof."

"Has anyone called Derek?" Sasha ignored his jibe.

"I called him after the hospital first called me," Mom said. "I'll call him again to see where he's at." She opened her phone and stepped outside to call Sasha's fiancé.

5

"You had me worried for a while," Caleb said.

"Why?"

"We only heard you'd had an accident and were in surgery. We didn't know how serious that would be."

"Hopefully I'll be back to normal by October in time for the wedding."

"It's only April. Should be plenty of time."

"What day is it?" Sasha strained to lift her head with a sudden urgency. "Caleb, quick. What day is it?"

"It's still Wednesday. The same day you had the accident. Calm down. You haven't been asleep for long."

"I was supposed to pick Alanah up from Spokane airport tonight. Caleb. What time is it?"

He flicked a glance at his watch. "Just after six ... Alanah?"

"Alanah Walker. You remember her, from high school in Australia."

Remember her. Just the sound of her name sent rockets of emotion soaring through his system. A shaft of guilt stabbed. This was what he should have felt last night when he'd proposed to Kyla.

"You have to go and get her." Sasha cut off his internal dialogue. "I promised I'd be there to meet her when she arrived."

"What time was her flight due in?"

"About half an hour ago. Caleb, she's going to be frantic. This is her first time out of Australia, and I promised I'd be there."

Caleb did a quick calculation. It was nearly three hours from Walla Walla to Spokane. She was going to be wandering around a strange foreign airport wondering what had happened.

"Get Mom to call her and let her know I'm on my way."

"She wasn't going to use her Australian cell here. We were going to buy a SIM for her to use in the US, but I don't have that number yet."

"Honestly, Sasha. Get Mom to call the airport and get a message to her."

"Go, Caleb. Stop fussing. She needs to see a familiar face."

Caleb resisted rolling his eyes. Fussing? Said the pot calling the kettle black.

Less than ten minutes later, Caleb was on the highway north to Spokane. Familiar face. If only Sasha knew. How come he hadn't heard Alanah was arriving so soon? How did he feel about it now that he knew? Warm, fuzzy, excited. Wrong, wrong, wrong. Those were the wrong feelings. Those were the feelings he should have been feeling last night with Kyla.

He was jolted from his emotional reflection by the buzzing on his smart watch, then the car screen lit up with an incoming call. Kyla. The warm and fuzzy feeling fizzled as guilt poured all over his thoughts.

"Hi." Guilt, not gladness. This was not good.

"Hey, Caleb. What are we doing tonight?"

Had he said they would do something tonight? Not that he could remember. But they were newly engaged. He supposed it was a reasonable assumption.

"Sorry, Kyla. I've got an emergency I have to deal with tonight."

"What's happened?"

"Sasha had an accident and has broken her leg in a couple of places."

"Caleb. That's awful. Is she going to be all right?"

"She's had surgery, and the doctor said she'll recover after PT and stuff."

"You sound like you're driving. Are you on your way to the hospital? Do you want me to come?"

Another shaft of guilt. He hadn't even thought to include Kyla in his response to the crisis. This was not a good start along the road to one heart, one flesh.

"I'm actually driving to Spokane—"

7

"Oh, no. Was it that bad? I'm so sorry."

"No, Sasha's in the hospital at Walla Walla, but I'm driving to meet her friend who's arriving tonight from Australia."

"Oh." The silence that followed was heavy and ominous.

"Sasha was supposed to meet her as soon as she arrived, and she needs to see a familiar face as this is her first time out of her own country."

"Well, what's the use in you going? She could have caught the bus down, couldn't she?"

"First of all, traveling internationally alone is a big deal, especially landing in a foreign country—"

"I assume she landed in LA first, didn't she? She's managed to get that far. Surely, she could catch the bus."

"Sasha promised she would meet her."

"Well, that's Sasha—her friend—and now she can't. I can't see why you need to go. What difference will it make?"

"I'm Alanah's friend too."

A new and dangerous silence ensued. Was she still on the line, or had she disconnected?

"Was this the girlfriend you talked about from high school?"

"I don't remember talking about any girlfriends with you."

"I asked you a while ago if you'd ever had another relationship before us."

She had. And Caleb had mentioned a high school crush. But he hadn't thought he would ever see her again. Since he'd been thinking about her, he acknowledged that Alanah had been more than a crush. She was a close friend, and his feelings for her had been real and serious. Only the distance thing ...

"Is this the one?" Kyla's tone had an edge.

"Yes, this is the one, but I didn't know she was coming until today."

"Well, given the circumstances, I'm sure you shouldn't be the one to meet her. Get Lucy to go pick her up. Besides, I wanted to talk to you tonight about our future in church ministry."

"What ministry?" Caleb knew. Kyla hadn't made her ambitions any secret. She wanted to be a pastor's wife—a lead pastor's wife.

"Why do you always back away from moving forward? This is what God's called you to, right?"

Caleb felt himself withdraw. He'd studied for Christian ministry. He loved the idea of pastoring people, but he wasn't ready to push himself forward. Something about Kyla's ambition made him recoil. It didn't feel right. But she was determined.

"I will think about it, but let's talk later," he said. "My head's not in that space right now, with Sasha's accident and all."

"You mean going to meet Sasha's friend."

"And my friend. I think you should be secure enough to allow me to meet with an old mate without turning it into a federal case."

"There you go, being all Australian again."

"I'm not ashamed of the years we spent there as kids, and I don't appreciate your tone."

"Fine, Caleb. Go and meet her, but you better let her know where you stand. You have a fiancée now, and she better not expect you to pick up where you left off."

"We 'left off' by deciding there was no future in our relationship. She's Australian, I'm American. We live on opposite sides of the world. You should calm down, Kyla, and let me greet her as a friend."

Kyla's response was a tight "goodbye." Guilt knifed through Caleb again. She was so pushy, and, so it would appear, possessive. His jaw clenched as he thought about the exchange. He would consider a paid church ministry position when God made a way for him. He was not going to angle and manipulate to get one. And he would greet Alanah with joy, and not feel guilty.

———

HER FLIGHT HAD BEEN DELAYED. Alanah hoped Sasha had checked her messages, because it would be awful if she had to wait three hours for the flight from LAX to arrive. There wasn't anything Alanah could do about it now. She may as well sit back and try to enjoy this last leg of the journey. But honestly that was going to be difficult. She'd been cramped in economy for the last twenty-four hours or so, and right at this moment, she vowed she would never take this journey again.

Los Angeles Airport had been a chaotic nightmare. Coming from a tiny town on the edge of the outback, population four hundred, with literally miles of nothing but crops and sheep and an occasional farmhouse scattered about, to arrive at an airport that had half the population of the world heaving to and fro was an assault on her senses. She was exhausted trying to take it all in. At least airplane etiquette allowed her to sit quietly, face forward, with no expectation to engage in conversation with the woman sitting next to her. On one hand, she felt guilty. It wasn't the Aussie way to ignore someone in such close proximity. But she was exhausted and didn't think she could summon the energy to be friendly. In any case, the middle-aged woman dressed in business attire didn't look like she was desperate for conversation.

Once the plane had reached altitude and levelled out, Alanah put her seat back a whole three centimeters. It hardly made any difference to her head, which was swimming with tiredness, but lamenting the sardine-like conditions was too much mental energy to spend. She closed her eyes and leaned deeper into the seat in an effort to relax.

Caleb smiled at her. Smiled in such a warm and loving way she wanted to melt into his arms. Why had it taken them the whole of high school to decide they should be together? Was it the stupid, immature teasing from the other boys in her class, or was it Sasha? What would

Sasha say when she found out Alanah and Caleb were an item? More than an item. Alanah was madly in love with him, so when he leaned in to kiss her, she closed her eyes and waited for the delicious warm connection. But it didn't come as she was interrupted by someone tapping her on the shoulder. This was so inconvenient.

"Excuse me, ma'am."

Alanah's eyes flew open and she was back mid-air, squashed in her window seat. Her heart was hammering at a ridiculous rate. Was that because of the dream or because she'd been jerked awake?

"Would you like tea or coffee?" The flight attendant spoke and the woman next to her looked annoyed that she was taking so long to answer.

"Ah, yes. Okay. Could I have a coffee please?"

"Cream and sugar?"

"Yes please." She assumed by cream, they meant milk—or some sort of white liquid that was supposed to resemble milk. Nothing like the milk she brought into the farmhouse when it was her turn to milk the cows.

Coffee on her tray table, and the flight attendant having moved on, Alanah's thoughts turned to the dream. She hadn't consciously thought of Caleb in a while. She had deliberately forced her thoughts away from him—away from the euphoric night of their school formal, and especially away from the day he'd told her his family would return to the States. She had wanted to be angry with him for allowing her to get so close that she'd believed there was a beautiful future together for them. But he hadn't known about his grandfather's heart attack. He hadn't known his parents would make the sudden decision to end their Australian adventure. Did she believe that? Was he as heartbroken as she had been? Probably not. She'd not heard from him since he'd returned to Trinity Lakes. It obviously hadn't meant as much to him as it had to her.

"Are you from South Africa?" The woman next to her decided to break the silence.

Alanah gave a weak smile and shook her head. Since leaving the shores of Australia she'd been accused of being a Kiwi, a South African, and a Brit. That was what came of being from South Australia. Their accent tended to be a bit more rounded than the other states.

"I'm from Australia. It's my first time flying internationally."

"I love your accent," the woman said.

"I love yours."

The woman smiled and turned back to her device.

Being in a foreign country meant Alanah was going to have to accept that she was the one with the accent, not everyone else. Perhaps she should wear a sticker on her shirt—I'm speaking Australian.

Her short nap must have been longer than she realized, as it wasn't long before the captain announced they should prepare the cabin for landing. She stowed her tray table and put her seat upright. It wouldn't be long now until she saw Sasha. She couldn't wait. They had so many things planned over the next few months leading up to the wedding.

By the time the plane had taxied into the air bridge, Alanah was fully awake, every nerve popping with energy. She couldn't wait to end this journey and begin her time with Sasha and her family—and Caleb. She had to think about him as well, as she would surely see him sometime during her stay here. He and Sasha still lived at home with their folks, so seeing him was unavoidable. She hoped it wouldn't be awkward.

Thank goodness disembarking this flight didn't include going through customs and immigration. That had been a proper circus when she'd landed in LA. Now all she had to do was walk through the airbridge, find the luggage carrousel, and Sasha would be there.

"Thank you for flying with us." The flight attendant stood at the door of the plane. "Enjoy your stay in Washington State."

Alanah smiled. Her anticipation had increased, and she was full of nervous energy. She hadn't seen Sasha in eleven years except on video calls. She hoped she would recognize her.

CHAPTER TWO

Caleb found a parking spot in the multi-story parking garage and literally ran into the terminal. He had no idea where he would find Alanah. He'd start with the airline information desk. There were several people in line, but none of them looked remotely like the Alanah he'd known a decade ago. He got into the queue and checked the arrivals monitor while he waited. Oh, flip. The flight had been delayed three hours and had only just landed twenty minutes ago. She was probably at the luggage carousel waiting for Sasha.

Caleb scrambled to find the right area, and then checked the monitors for the correct carousel for the flight from LA. He'd worried he wouldn't recognize Alanah, but spotted her at once, standing like a lost child watching the suitcases trundle past. She was exactly the same, only more mature—and beautiful.

"Alanah."

She glanced up, evidently confused, and several other people in the crowd also turned to see who was calling loudly.

"Alanah." He waved and moved in her direction. It took a few seconds before she recognized him, but she didn't smile. She appeared stunned, and the people nearby were excusing to reach around her.

"Hey. Remember me? Caleb?"

Had she forgotten?

"I was supposed to meet Sasha."

That wonderful Aussie accent. He hadn't heard it in so long, and it brought back a flood of memories from his teenage years.

"I know." He came next to her and drew her aside from the pressing crowd. "She had an accident and is in hospital."

Alanah gasped and looked at him. "What? Is she all right?"

"She's broken her leg—badly—and had to have surgery. But she'll be okay."

Tears glistened in her eyes. He was an idiot. He shouldn't have blurted it out just like that.

"She's going to be all right. Don't worry." He put his arm around her shoulders, but instead of it being a quick squeeze of reassurance, she turned into his embrace like a lost soul—and it felt right. Love coursed through him like warm honey, and he didn't want to let go. But he had to. This wasn't right. It wasn't fair to Kyla. Or to Alanah.

"Let's get your bags." He broke the physical connection and turned towards the baggage carousels, but the cold sense of emptiness was almost a literal pain. "Has your luggage been around yet?"

Alanah mumbled something and pointed toward one of the last suitcases still doing the circuit.

"Is that yours?" Obviously, but he had to say something. This shocked silence was horrible.

Alanah walked over and grabbed the bag from the conveyor belt herself. Caleb smiled. She had always been an active, strong farm girl. And of course, she'd just been in at least two other airports on her own.

"Can I help?" He pointed to her large backpack and hoped he didn't sound condescending.

15

"Thanks." She handed him the backpack. She'd obviously used the full weight allowable, but then he'd flown internationally enough times to know you needed every ounce to pack everything but the kitchen sink on long-haul flights.

Caleb tried several sentences in his mind. He needed to say something—anything—to establish the ease of friendship they used to enjoy.

"Did you have a good trip?" That sounded safe and sensible.

"It was awful." Alanah looked like she might cry again. "I didn't realize how long it took to get all the way round the world."

"Tell me about it. I'm not keen to do that long flight again." And that was the wrong thing to say, because distance was the reason he'd broken it off with her in the first place. That beautiful warm starlit night, eleven years ago, when he'd asked Alanah to take a walk after Christmas dinner, he'd hoped she would leave Australia and follow him and his family back to Trinity Lakes. But that was a ridiculous idea. She was as attached to her family and home as he was to his.

"I'm sorry, Alanah. I didn't mean to be insensitive."

"That's okay. I'm just wrecked. All I want to do is lie down and sleep. Sleep flat, not cramped like a croissant in a lunch box."

Caleb laughed at the imagery.

"The bad news is we still have a two and a half hour's drive before we reach home."

Alanah's shoulders drooped further.

"Do you want to stop and get something to eat first?"

"Not really." She sounded sad.

"Do you mind if I grab something quickly? I didn't get time to eat dinner before being called to the hospital."

Alanah turned to face him a small frown creasing her brow. "I'm sorry, Caleb. I'm feeling sorry for myself. Let's get something to eat. I'm sure another half hour isn't going to change anything."

Caleb wanted to suggest going to a nice café to eat a proper meal, but she looked tired and disappointed that it was him and not Sasha, so he elected to drive through the nearest fast-food burger chain.

In the end, Alanah ordered a burger, fries, and milkshake. That was more like the girl he remembered.

————

ALANAH FELT BETTER ONCE she'd consumed some sugar. When Sasha had been a no-show, she'd been anxious, worried that she had landed in a strange place with no one to meet her. She'd logged into the airport's Wi-Fi and sent Sasha a message but didn't get a reply. Then her name had been announced over the PA system and she'd gone to the information desk near the gate lounge. Mrs. Kennedy had left a message to say Sasha would be a couple of hours late, but obviously the message had got tangled in communication because Sasha didn't appear at all. Instead, it was Caleb who called her name in the middle of a crowd. It had taken her forever to get all the pieces together. Sasha was not going to come at all. Caleb was there in Sasha's place, looking as handsome as ever, and putting his arm around her shoulders. How embarrassing. She'd responded to the hug as if they were still close, like all those years ago. But he'd pulled away quickly. She'd known it was finished ages ago.

She hadn't expected to find anything of their mutual attraction still alive, but here it was, pulsing and sparking with a depth she'd not experienced since he'd left.

"I see you've grown a beard." This was supposed to be a start to safe small talk, but all it did was draw her attention to how good he looked with a short-cut beard, wearing a baseball cap with his pullover.

"Too lazy to shave all the time." He gave a killer smile as he felt the growth on his chin. This was so not a safe place to start small talk.

"Tell me more about Sasha's accident." Alanah slurped the last of her thick shake through the straw.

"She was helping clean gutters on one of the cabins at the summer campground and fell off the roof."

"She's such a clown. Honestly."

"I wonder if Derek knows what he's getting himself into," Caleb said. "She's always doing something outlandish."

"She's not usually accident prone though, is she?" Alanah asked. "I remember us getting into all sorts of difficult situations, but we usually got through without too many scrapes and bruises."

"It's great to see you again," Caleb said. "Sasha hadn't told me you were coming until this afternoon at the hospital."

"You knew I was coming for the wedding, right?"

"I'd heard you might, but that's four months away."

"I decided to take a trip and do some sightseeing. I've never been out of Australia before."

"Great. Where are you going to go?"

"Canada, mostly. I'm an *Anne of Green Gables* fan from way back and have to see Prince Edward Island."

"Never heard of it."

Alanah shot him a glare. "You have too. Sasha and I watched *Anne of Green Gables* a million times when we were at school, and you used to tease us about it."

Caleb smiled. "I didn't watch it, though," he said. "Even if I had, it doesn't follow I'd know about Prince Henry Island."

"Prince Edward, and since you insist on being daft, it's on the East Coast, not far from Boston."

"Right. I shall not forget." He threw a smile in her direction again. "Will you go to Boston while you're on the East Coast?"

"And New York. Then we're coming back west and doing Banff and the whole glass-topped train thing."

"We?"

"Me and Sasha."

"When do you plan to go?"

"Straight after summer camp. Me and Sasha have registered as camp counselors for a couple of weeks."

Caleb was quiet and bit his lip.

"You don't think she'll be able to go?"

"Based on what the doctor said, she definitely won't be doing summer camp, and I doubt she'll be able to go touring around the country—unless you want to push her in a wheelchair."

Caleb's words were like a punch in the gut. All the things she and Sasha had planned—possibly weren't going to happen.

———

AS SOON AS he'd mentioned Sasha's prognosis, the light-hearted conversation had crashed. Caleb hated being the bearer of bad news.

"I guess we'd better get on the road," he said. Alanah nodded and threw her wrappers in the trash.

Caleb didn't know what to say once they were back on the highway. It was obvious that Alanah was gutted by the news of Sasha's accident, and what that might mean for her plans. It was going to be a long drive if he didn't turn her focus to something else.

"What have you been doing for work since you left school?"

"I went to uni and did a degree in social work, but I haven't used it. I'm working at the local council in admin."

"It's so strange, hearing the Aussie lingo after all these years."

"Your accent is the same. What have you been up to?"

"I went to college and did a couple of years towards a music degree, but then came back to Trinity Lakes to Bible college, focusing on pastoral ministry."

"Wow. So you're a pastor now?"

Caleb smiled. "No. I work part-time at a music store and tutor music students."

"Pastoring not for you then?"

"I am one of the youth leaders at our church, but only in a volunteer capacity at this stage."

"Would you like for it to be full-time?"

"Not sure." Not sure? Even tonight, Kyla had been pushing for him to be more ambitious within the church. He still couldn't fathom the reason why he'd been reluctant to join her enthusiasm, but did he want to be a pastor or not? Kyla seemed to think it was a foregone conclusion—well, she had plans on how she wanted his life to go. At this moment, he wasn't so sure.

Alanah had gone quiet again.

"You had always talked about doing something with people." Caleb glanced her way.

"There's not much opportunity in the way of paid positions out bush."

"You don't want to move to the city?"

"I hated living there when I was at uni. I couldn't wait to get back home. The bush is in my blood, and I still love the farm. I help Dad and Mitch out whenever I can. I should have been a farmer."

Caleb wanted to smile. This was who she was. But it also reconfirmed why they could never be together. If she wouldn't move to the city, she'd be even less likely to move halfway around the world—even if she still loved him.

What was he thinking? He was engaged to someone else.

"I got engaged recently." He blurted it out.

"Oh." Alanah sounded stunned.

Why did he feel as if he'd just stuck a lance into her heart?

"Kyla and I have been going out for a couple of years, and I finally asked her to marry me."

"That's great, Caleb. Congratulations." Her tone didn't match her words. Was she upset by the news? It didn't make any difference if she was upset. They had agreed eleven years ago that they weren't right for each other.

Several miles passed before Caleb noticed a difference in the silence. He glanced across the car. Alanah had fallen asleep. That was for the best. Their conversation was doomed by the unresolvable obstacle standing between them. He still had feelings for her, and it seemed possible that she still felt something for him as well. If only they'd been born in the same town, or the same state, or even the same country.

There was no future in dwelling on this. He'd asked Kyla to be his wife, and he needed to school his emotions to follow that joyous path. Alanah was his happy past, not his future.

CHAPTER THREE

Alanah had been embarrassed when she woke just as they arrived at the Kennedy's home, on the outskirts of Trinity Lakes. The outside light was on. Her phone said it was nearly one a.m., but her watch wasn't connected to the internet, and was still on Adelaide time. So was her jetlagged brain. It was almost 6:30 p.m. at home. Time for dinner. No wonder she was hungry.

"Alanah." Marianne Kennedy came out to the driveway in her dressing gown and slippers. They must have waited up for her to arrive. "You must be exhausted after your flight. Do you want a cup of hot chocolate before you go to bed?"

Alanah received the warm hug that Mrs. Kennedy offered. "I'm ashamed to say I slept most of the drive from the airport. I've been poor company for Caleb." She watched as he lifted her suitcase and backpack from the back of his ute—no, truck. Mental note. She was in America now.

"Well, we'd love to share a hot drink with you before going to bed, if you're up for it."

Alanah nodded. Hopefully she could get some food as well. "It's good to see you, Mrs. Kennedy."

"Please call me Marianne. High school days are long gone."

Alanah smiled. High school days were long gone. But it seemed strange calling her history teacher by her first name.

As Caleb came by, Alanah reached out to take her luggage from him.

"Let Caleb bring it in, Alanah," Marianne said. "You come through to the kitchen and let's get some milk warmed for you."

"Sorry." Alanah smiled at Caleb as he hefted the bags into the house.

"It's my pleasure." He smiled back.

"I'm so sorry Sasha wasn't there to meet you at the airport," Marianne said as she continued into the house. "Did you get my message?"

"I did, but it was a bit confused. Doesn't matter. Caleb found me and got me here safely."

"I can't believe she was on a roof, cleaning gutters," Marianne said.

"I usually help Mitch clean gum leaves from the gutters at the beginning of every fire season."

"Yes, but you don't usually fall off the roof," Caleb said as he entered the kitchen.

"You assume I don't." Alanah smiled at him.

Caleb laughed.

"How is Michele?" Marianne asked.

"Mitch? He hates going by the name Michele."

"He was always so lively when I taught him in history class."

"I bet he was, if you kept calling him Michele," Caleb said as he sat at the table with his hot drink.

"By lively, I guess you mean the class clown," Alanah said. "He's good. Left school as soon as he was allowed to and came home to work on the farm."

"Speaking of history class, we've got our annual Anzac Day festival on Saturday."

Alanah did a double take. "You celebrate Anzac Day here?"

"Not in most parts of the country, but since James and I spent so many years teaching in Australia and New Zealand, we've brought back a few bits of culture and included them in our history curriculum."

"Yeah, Dad has been teaching Australian Rules football in gym class ever since we returned," Caleb said. "We'll have an exhibition AFL match on Saturday to add to all things Australian."

"Wow. Really?"

"It's not like the professional football you guys play in Australia, but it resembles it."

"Caleb is the star player." Marianne placed a cup of hot chocolate on the breakfast bar in front of Alanah. "Do you want a cookie?"

"Yes, please." A biscuit would be just the thing to keep the wolves at bay.

"I had the advantage of playing Aussie rules football all my teen years," Caleb said. "Most of the guys who play have only taken it up in high school as part of the gym program. Some of them are keen."

"No budding stars among them?" Alanah asked.

"I don't think they send scouts this far to find players." Caleb grinned at her.

"I'm glad you got here in time," Marianne said. "It will be great to have another Australian in our midst when we hold the last post ceremony."

"So, this is when? Saturday?"

Marianne nodded.

"But today is the twenty-fifth of April."

Caleb laughed. "No, it's the twenty-fourth. Don't forget we're almost a day behind."

Alanah's brain swam. She'd flown east over the international date line and gained a day. It was all too hard to calculate, especially with jet lag doing its thing.

"Actually, it's now past midnight, so it is April twenty-fifth, but we don't have a national holiday to celebrate like you do in Australia. So we schedule our Anzac Day on the nearest Saturday."

"How many years have you been doing this?"

"Mom pitched the idea to the town committee after she'd been teaching First World War history for a couple of years."

"America didn't enter the war until 1917. As I loved your country and your Anzac Day traditions, I thought it would be great to teach as part of our First World War history unit. I held a small ceremony at school for a couple of years, but it has expanded in the last five years."

"And now we play footy," Caleb said.

"And eat Anzac cookies." Marianne smiled as she placed a plate of the familiar oatmeal and coconut biscuits on the kitchen bench. The biscuits were a traditional part of Alanah's childhood.

Alanah took a bite of her golden biscuit and washed it down with a mouth of hot chocolate. This was weird. The Kennedys had always had an American accent, but here they were, in their own American context, talking about one of Australia's most celebrated traditions. Talk about brain fudge.

———

"LANI." Alanah was sure Sasha's loud and enthusiastic greeting would have been heard throughout the entire ward. But she couldn't deny her poor injured friend, trussed up like a trebuchet ready to launch, holding her arms out in desperation.

"What have you done to yourself?"

"I was trying out a new look for the wedding."

"If you think I'm going to go for something matching as your bridesmaid, you can forget it."

Sasha laughed.

"It's so good to see you, Sash." Alanah hugged her friend, even though it was awkward negotiating the medical equipment.

"It's taken you eleven years to get on a plane to come and see me. Don't leave it that long again, Lani."

"It's all right for you to say. It's taken me eleven years to save enough to get here. Besides, the planes fly both ways you know."

"Come here." Sasha held out her arms again, and Alanah responded with a second warm hug.

"Thanks for meeting me at the airport." Alanah pulled up a visitor's chair and sat close enough to hold her friend's hand.

"I'm so sorry. I was all set to leave the working party in time to meet your flight, then the next thing I know, I'm waking up post-surgery. I freaked out when I realized."

"My plane was delayed, so I only missed Caleb by about ten minutes, and he found me in the baggage claim area." Even as she said his name, Alanah couldn't help the mix of emotions that churned her stomach.

"Thank goodness he loves me so much he'll drop everything to get me out of a fix."

Alanah nodded. Of course Caleb had rushed to pick her up because he loved his sister, but Alanah wished it had been because he loved her. Stop it! There was nothing to be gained by indulging in that old fairy tale. She'd kissed him eleven years ago—and loved it. And that had been that. Relationship over.

"So Caleb's engaged." Time to focus on the facts.

"What?" Sasha's forehead creased with a frown. "Who told you that?"

"He did. On the drive home last night."

"Who to?"

Alanah shrugged. He'd probably said his fiancée's name, but she couldn't remember it. She'd been too involved with her own sinking feeling of loss to pay too much attention.

"I bet he's gone and proposed to Kyla."

"Who's Kyla?"

"Caleb's 'girlfriend'." She used air quotes.

"You don't sound like you're a fan."

"I'm not."

"Why? If Caleb likes her ..."

"I don't know, Lani. She's not like you, that's for sure."

A jolt of alarm shot through Alanah. Had Caleb told his sister about their brief Christmas romance?

"There was a time when I thought he might go out with you," Sasha continued.

"We did sort of go out a bit, right at the end of school."

"I know he took you home from the formal, but I would hardly call that going out."

Did Alanah want to admit to the depths of how far she'd fallen in love with Sasha's brother? Better not. It was history. Time to change the subject.

"Why don't you like Kyla? What's she like?"

"She's all right, I suppose. She's attractive enough, I guess, and works with Caleb with our youth group. It's just ..."

"Just what?"

"I don't know. I'm not sure she's what I want for my brother."

"Do you think you really have a say in it?"

"He's my twin. If he hadn't liked Derek, I'm not sure I would have agreed to marry him."

"Really? Poor Derek. Does he know?"

Sasha nodded. "Yeah. Derek knows, and he's very understanding. Luckily, he and Caleb get along like a house on fire, so there's no issue."

"I'm glad." Glad that Sasha and Derek had worked out. Not so glad that she and Caleb hadn't.

"Anyway—you're here." Sasha gave a girly squeal as if they

were thirteen and still in high school. "I've been so excited about all the things we've planned."

"Me too …" Alanah paused. All the things they'd planned, and here was Sasha, her full leg in some sort of support cast apparatus and suspended on a pulley system that would rival anything in the farm shed.

"What?" Sasha frowned. "What's with that tone?"

"We're off to summer camp in little over a week." Alanah waved her hand in the direction of the oversized, immobile limb. "How are you going to manage?"

Now Sasha frowned. "It's so stupid. I was fine until the wind blew that branch. And it was only a tap—a tap! How stupid that I should lose my balance and tumble off the roof."

"O, H, and S fail."

"What?"

"Occupational, health, and safety. You know—the government department that monitors every little thing in the workplace to make sure you don't fall from the top of a cabin?"

"Oh, right. We call it OSHA."

"So many acronyms."

"Yeah, well, I guess I'm not going to mention it, because I didn't exactly plan how I was going to clean the gutters, and I suppose there must be a host of safety precautions I should have taken but didn't. I don't want to sue the campground."

"Anyhow, will you be mobile in ten days time? We have a week of training activities. Are you even going to be able to come on summer camp?"

"The doctor was talking about discharge from hospital on Saturday."

"What will you be allowed to do? I can't see you being allowed to get involved in all the camp activities."

"I can sing around a campfire—probably."

"But what about the hiking and canoeing and rock climbing?"

Sasha's shoulders deflated and her lips rolled in on themselves.

"Will it be okay if we're one counselor down for the outside activities?" Alanah asked.

"Alanaaah." Sasha's eyes held pleading. "I wanted to come with you and remember all the times we used to kick around as kids."

"Check with the doctor and see what he says."

"Says about what?" Caleb walked into the hospital room holding flowers.

"You bought me flowers." Sasha brightened as Caleb dumped the flowers on her lap.

"Not really. Kyla bought them and asked me to send her love."

Sasha rolled her eyes, and Alanah cast a worried glance in Caleb's direction. His sister's disapproval was obvious. Would he tell his sister about the engagement now? She waited. No. Nothing. Why hadn't he told her?

"What are you asking the doctor about?" Caleb continued as if the subject of Kyla and the flowers was finished.

"Will she be able to be a camp counselor in a week and a half?" Alanah said.

"I doubt it," he said. "When I had surgery on my ankle, I wasn't allowed to do anything useful for several weeks, and even then, it was after a heap of PT."

"PT?" Alanah asked.

"Physio," Caleb said. Right. Of course.

Alanah watched Sasha's response at this news. Downcast and miserable.

"Perhaps you could come and help lead the discussion groups and campfire singing, like you said." Alanah hoped to see that her encouragement had worked.

"They'll have to find a replacement because there has to be a

29

certain ratio of leaders to campers when conducting activities."
Sasha lifted her gaze to her brother.

"What? Wait. No. I'm not going to any summer camp."

"Please, Caleb. I'll do all the sitting around in circles singing
'Kumbaya.' You just need to help facilitate the activities."

"I have work, Sasha. If I don't work, I don't get paid."

"Half your music students will be at camp. Who are you
going to teach?"

"It's not summer vacation yet, and the first week is leader
training, isn't it?" Caleb argued.

"Please. Elaine will want to support the summer camp. I
know she will."

Alanah wanted to ask who Elaine was, but Sasha had that
silent challenge hanging in the air, waiting for Caleb to cave.

"I will ask Kyla …"

"Kyla. What's she got to do with it?" Sasha's tone was
explosive.

"She's one of the youth group leaders with me, and I'm sure
she will want to help out."

"But I want you to come. Not Kyla."

Alanah wished she could run down the hall for a quick bathroom break. These two were intense.

"Elaine may give me a couple of afternoons off to help out,
but Kyla is more likely to be able to adjust her schedule." He
grabbed his phone and stepped toward the door. "I'll make a
couple of phone calls."

"Wow." Alanah let out a full lung of air she'd been holding
while the siblings had been standing off against each other.

"He'll come," Sasha said. "He loves the outdoor activities and
working with kids."

"But we don't get paid. Only a small allowance, plus food
and accommodation."

"He's still living at home. He'll manage so long as Elaine will
let him have some time."

Alanah smiled. Just like high school. The three of them hanging out together. Was she glad or concerned?

"He better not send Kyla," Sasha said.

"You might have to learn to like her, Sash. She's going to be your sister soon."

Sasha flopped back against her pillows and let out a loud sigh. "I wish it were you."

CHAPTER FOUR

Anzac Day. Well, it wasn't really, being the twenty-ninth of April, but she'd missed the day of memorial while she flew across the international date line, so this was as near as she would get. Obviously, today's football game and short memorial service was not the full, national day of dawn services, street marches, and stadiums full of people observing a minute's silence.

"I guess I'll get to see the way the Americans do these things come Independence Day," Alanah said to Marianne as they carried containers of biscuits towards the food tables set up at the side of the sports field.

"We celebrate Memorial Day on the last Monday in May. That's more like the feel of your Australian Anzac Day."

The sports field was square, not like the ovals that were at all schools and communities around Australia. There were modest bleachers set around the four sides of the field. Obviously, they played American football here as well. However, today the four posts particular for Aussie rules were at either end. It looked different in a square rather than oval setting.

"So you and Mr. Kennedy introduced this as part of the student curriculum?"

Marianne nodded. "The town organizing committee have jumped on board, particularly because there are several other expats in town who find this small piece of Aussie culture a dose of home."

"Mrs. Kennedy." Alanah stopped as Marianne waited for the young woman who'd called out to them. "Hi." The young woman addressed Alanah. "I'm Selena Palis, journalist with the Trinity Lakes Gazette."

"Hi," Alanah replied.

Marianne turned toward Alanah with a smile. "I told Selena you'd be here today, and she thought it might be interesting to do an interview with you about how Anzac Day is celebrated in Australia."

"I wouldn't say it's celebrated," Alanah said. "It's a national day of memorial."

"Right. Like our Memorial Day?"

"Apparently." Alanah looked towards Marianne for confirmation.

"Can you tell me about Anzac Day in Australia?" Selena asked. "Sorry, I should have asked if it was okay to do an interview. Would you mind?"

"No, that would be fine, I think. Is that okay with you?" Alanah asked Marianne.

"Have you got time to go to the Bellbird Café for a coffee?" Marianne asked, and they all consulted their watches.

"No. Nearly time for the ceremony," Selena said. "I don't want to miss it, since it's so important to Jason."

"Then you girls go ahead and chat. I've got to talk to Vanessa Wainscott to make sure we've got morning tea all ready to go." Marianne moved away, and Alanah followed Selena to a nearby school bench.

"Mrs. Wainscott is going to be my grandmother in-law soon," Selena said. "Her grandson, my fiancé, is Australian."

"Really? Where's he from?"

"I want to say Victoria. That's a state, right?"

Alanah nodded. "Country or city?"

"Melbourne. Jason tells me it's the sporting and cultural capital of Australia."

Alanah laughed. "You're talking to the wrong person. I'm from South Australia, and there's huge rivalry between our two states."

"Are you telling me Melbourne isn't the capital?" Selena had her stylus poised over her tablet.

"The government capital is Canberra. As to sporting capital —I guess we have to concede because of the number of international sporting events Melbourne hosts, but Adelaide would like to challenge on a number of points."

"You don't feel strongly about this, then?" Selena smiled.

"What gave it away?"

"I'd say the raised hackles and fiery eyes. Have you met my fiancé, Jason?"

"Not yet," Alanah said, "but we can go head-to-head on which state is better. I'd win."

"Jason told me Victoria is the only state that's habitable. The rest is just outback."

"Your Jason and I are going to get along famously, I can see."

Selena raised questioning eyebrows.

"South Australia is mostly outback, but the settled areas around the coast are productive, beautiful, and our capital city has been in the top five most livable cities in the world many times running."

"I'd like to see the outback," Selena said.

Alanah smiled. The outback was apparently quite famous. She didn't know why. There was nothing there, except Uluru, a lot of red dirt, and a load of cattle.

34

"Tell me about Anzac Day in Australia." Selena focused back on the task at hand.

"It starts with a dawn service—the service actually starts half an hour before dawn and finishes as the sun rises. They play the 'Last Post' on a bugle, observe a minute's silence, and then put the flags back from half-mast."

"Flags?"

"Australian and New Zealand. Sometimes the British Union Jack as well."

"And that's it? A memorial service before dawn?"

Alanah laughed. "No, then all the veterans from all the wars, plus children and grandchildren of veterans who are no longer with us, march in a parade, wearing their ancestors' war medals."

"And then that's it?"

"No. Then the veterans go to the pub to catch up with mates they fought with, those who are still alive. They play a game of two-up."

"I think Mrs. Kennedy has a couple of exhibition rounds of two-up today."

"It's iconic, and associated with the vets getting together."

"Then that's the end of the day?"

"No, then everyone expects to watch the afternoon football match. The major game always has the crowd observe a minute's silence and the last post, and then the game."

"And the Anzac cookies?"

"Anzac biscuits. Yes. They're the traditional biscuits that loved ones baked and sent in tins across to their soldiers on the front. Made of oatmeal, golden syrup, and coconut."

"I tasted some of the batch Mrs. Wainscott was making."

"I'm amazed that Trinity Lakes holds this day," Alanah said.

"From what I've learned of Trinity Lakes, they are a community who love town festivals. The Kennedy family brought back this little bit of Australian culture, and the town took to it. I know Jason loves having something from his home to connect with. And really, it's not so strange."

"What do you mean?"

"We celebrate the Irish on Saint Patrick's Day, and there are always Italian, German, and other cultural festivals being celebrated around the country. People love a bit of international culture."

"Just one more thing to note in your article. Many of us watch the Anzac dawn services held at Gallipoli and Villers-Bretonneux in France."

"They hold Anzac in Gall-where?"

"Gallipoli. It's in Turkey, and where the Anzac legend began. It was a failed military operation where over eight thousand Australian and New Zealand soldiers were killed. It was a disaster from start to finish, but it was where the Australian and New Zealand troops formed bonds that have lasted over a hundred years. The dawn services there are very emotional, as you see representatives from Turkey, New Zealand, and Australia pay respect to the fallen from all sides."

"Wow. That sounds … like … I mean it sounds like there has been some forgiveness and reconciliation."

"Hey, Alanah." Alanah turned to see Caleb pushing Sasha in a wheelchair. She waved.

"Hey, Sel," Sasha said as they approached.

"Are you playing today?" Selena asked Caleb.

He nodded. "Is Jason playing?"

"He is, though he's complaining about it."

"Why?" Sasha said. "I thought, as an Aussie, he'd love to be involved in an Australian Rules football game."

"Tell him to stop complaining," Caleb said. "He knows how to play, and we need him."

"Alex Sinclair and Joel Manning are also playing. Another couple of Aussies," Selena said.

"Where're they from?" Alanah asked.

"Alex is a rugby man from Queensland," Caleb said. "Joel's not been in the area long, but I think he's from Sydney, so presumably he's a rugby man as well."

"Perhaps you guys should have made it a rugby match instead of AFL."

"No, it has to be AFL. That's the game Dad brought back from Australia and has been teaching in gym class all these years. This began as part of the school curriculum, and has sort of grown from there. We have so many locals playing AFL now that we've organized a small competition."

"Anyway, Alanah," Sasha said, "can I get you to take over wheeling me around the place? Caleb has to get ready for the game."

"Sure." Alanah smiled.

Caleb parked Sasha's chair next to the bench and stepped aside.

"Thanks, Alanah." Caleb's smile in her direction set off an electric shock in her stomach which launched right through her chest into her throat.

"Got a thing for Caleb, have you?" Selena asked, once he'd walked away.

"What? No." Alanah felt blood rush to her face.

Selena smiled and raised her eyebrows. "No one would blame you if you did."

"Except maybe Kyla." Sasha's statement was laced with annoyance.

"Caleb and I went to school together." It was best if she put this journalist off the scent. "We go way back. We're just friends."

Selena smiled again. "If you say so."

Selena clearly didn't believe her. And now Sasha had a knowing smirk on her face.

"Just friends. You know this, Sasha, so you needn't look at me in that tone of voice."

Both girls laughed.

"Besides, he's engaged."

Sasha mumbled something under her breath, unintelligible, but Alanah guessed it wasn't anything complimentary about Caleb's new fiancée.

———

"Selena seems nice," Alanah said, once they had finished and she was pushing Sasha closer to the playing field.

"She's new in town, but yeah, she seems nice." Sasha replied. "Uh oh."

"What?"

"Ten o'clock. Kyla Ferguson."

"Caleb's Kyla?" Alanah scanned the direction indicated, though Sasha had taken hold of the wheels and was trying to steer in the opposite direction. There was a young woman. Quite tall and spindly. Dark hair tied in a bouncy ponytail. She appeared nice enough, except for the scowl on her face.

"Hey, Sasha," Kyla called across the distance. Alanah stopped pushing and allowed the woman to catch up.

"Hi, I'm Kyla. Caleb's fiancée." She thrust a hand in Alanah's direction and Alanah responded. The handshake was firm and seemed friendly, but the expression on her face didn't match the handshake. There was a challenge in her eyes. "You're Sasha's friend from Australia," Kyla said.

Alanah nodded.

"She's Caleb's friend too," Sasha said.

"Yes, he told me all about you."

Alanah felt herself blushing. What had he said? Was Kyla always aggressive or was this display put on for her benefit?

"He told me you needed help filling your role as camp counselor." Kyla turned her focus on Sasha.

38

"Yes, I hoped he'd be able to help with the outdoor activities. As you can see, I'm not going to be much good for a while."

"He asked me, but I'd already registered. I was going to be there anyway."

"Oh?" Sasha didn't sound pleased.

"But the youth committee had a quick meeting and decided to sponsor Caleb so he can take the time off work. We had some money in an emergency fund and had already used some to sponsor Justin Perry to come, so we thought it would be cool to have all our youth leaders be part of the team. I guess you won't need to come now."

Was Kyla addressing her or Sasha?

"We'll both be going," Sasha said. "Alanah and I have been planning this for nearly a year, and there's no way I'm going to miss out."

"I'm sure that will be nice. I hope it doesn't cause too much disruption to the program. Perhaps it would be better if your friend stayed at home with you." She was speaking to Sasha but indicated Alanah. "Caleb and I will be able to make up the difference."

"No. You were already signed up. They were expecting both Alanah and me, so we'll still both go. It will be great having my brother there as well. It will be a great opportunity for him to catch up with Alanah after all these years. They were great friends, you know."

Alanah nearly exploded. What was Sasha doing? Deliberately provoking Kyla, that's what. What on earth? Alanah squeezed Sasha's shoulder.

"It will be good to get to know you too, Kyla," Alanah said. "Caleb told me all about you. You must be thrilled to be engaged."

"Yes. I am."

There was no mistaking her tone—back off, chickadee. Well,

Alanah had no intention of trespassing on Kyla's sacred ground, so she could take the hostility out of her tone.

As Kyla walked away, Sasha took hold of the wheels and tried to propel herself toward the stands, but didn't get very far.

"Have patience," Alanah said. "What's your hurry?"

"I'm upset," Sasha replied.

"Oh. That's what the steam coming from your ears is about." Alanah took the handles of the wheelchair and set Sasha into motion. "You shouldn't provoke her like that, Sash."

"Like what?" Sasha half turned her head back to talk.

"You know very well. Kyla feels insecure about me, and you deliberately mentioned our former friendship."

"What former? You and Caleb still get along well together. You're still friends."

"Stop it, Sasha. Caleb and I haven't spoken for eleven years."

"You spoke for several hours the other night."

"Sasha." Alanah tried to keep the frustration from her tone. "Kyla needs to feel secure in her relationship with your brother, and you're not helping."

Sasha fell silent, but Alanah wasn't convinced that she was repentant.

"Don't use me to cause trouble with Kyla and Caleb," Alanah said in a firm tone. "I love Caleb as a friend, but nothing more could ever develop between us. Besides, he's already chosen Kyla." Alanah parked the wheelchair in a spot designated for wheelchairs on the side of the football field.

"That is a very strange thing to say," Sasha said.

"What's strange?"

"You said nothing more could ever develop between you. Have you thought this through? Is it something you've considered?"

"What? No! I mean—"

"Alanah." Sasha's tone drew out her disbelief. "You have thought about Caleb as more than a friend, haven't you?"

"Is this relevant? Oh, look. They're assembling around the flagpole."

"Tell me." Sasha's tone was bossy and demanding. "When did you first think of him in that way?"

"Really? You want to talk about high school crushes now?"

"You crushed on him in high school?"

"Every teenage girl in the district crushed on him, except for you and your sisters."

"But why did you mention it now?"

"I didn't! You mentioned it. You're the one whose mind is always running to the romantic possibilities."

"So you haven't thought about Caleb as a possibility?" Sasha had turned the chair enough so that she now had Alanah in a solid glare. What was she supposed to say?

"Can we talk about this later? You're right. There is something in the past, but I don't want you dragging it out for all and sundry to comment on."

Sasha smiled. "I knew it."

Alanah rolled her eyes. Sasha was probably already processing romantic possibilities, but she was going to have to understand that she and Caleb had already been down all the different forks in the road, and they all led to one thing. It wasn't going to happen.

CHAPTER FIVE

"I still can't believe the players don't wear helmets and shoulder pads."

Caleb laughed at Selena Palis's statement.

"Alex plays rugby, and they don't wear any protective gear either," Caleb said. "And rugby is rougher than Aussie rules."

"But it's all so fast moving. And heavy tackling. And no helmets."

Caleb laughed again. "Don't quote this small exhibition match as your final opinion on how AFL is played. Search it up online and watch the professionals. It is a whole lot more skillful than what you saw today."

Selena scribbled a few more notes.

"Thanks for helping me out with the interview. I can't wait to visit Australia."

"You'll love it, especially if you go to where Jason comes from. Great coffee culture."

"So he keeps telling me. And you lived in the south when you were over there?" Selena asked.

"South Australia. It has no bearing or resemblance to what is called 'the South' here in the States. Completely different culture, climate, and landscape."

"I'm obviously going to have to do more research." Selena closed the cover on her tablet and put it in her bag. "Do you think you'll go back and visit South Australia when Alanah goes home?"

What? Where did that question come from? And why did it nearly knock him from his perch?

"I … ah …"

"No need to explain. I get it." Selena gave a smile that could have been interpreted as knowing. Knowing. What did she get? But she'd already left the locker room, and anything he said now would sound ridiculous.

But go back to Booleroo Whim? The often dry, dusty, one-horse town on the edge of the outback? Why did that thought sound appealing? Alanah. Well, that wasn't going to happen. Kyla would have a pink fit if he even suggested going Down Under. Stop it. The past was in the past. His future was with Kyla.

Despite his best efforts at self-talk, he was still thinking about Booleroo Whim and the happy years he'd spent there during high school when Kyla marched into the locker room.

"You all right?" She came and stood in front of him. "I don't think you'd better play this game anymore."

Caleb snapped from his daydreaming and stood up. "What are you talking about?"

"It's a dangerous game, and here you are still not recovered. I think it would be best if this were your last game."

"I'm perfectly all right." Caleb turned and shoved his football guernsey and boots into his sports bag. Who did she think she was, taking away permission for him to play a sport he loved?

"There's no need to get all defensive. I'm just concerned about you. That's all."

Caleb stopped, his sports bag in hand, and stared her in the eye. He knew he was frowning, but Kyla was talking to him as if she were his mother. It was annoying.

"Darling." Kyla stepped over to him and put her hand on his chest. "I hated seeing you play today."

"Why?" His frown did not lessen, despite the batting eyelids she sent in his direction.

"My heart was in my mouth every time you were grabbed and thrown to the ground."

Thrown to the ground? Tackled. She made it sound like he was a little kid being bullied.

"Tackling is part of the game, Kyla, and for your information, I shrugged most of the tackles and only got caught four times."

"I don't like it, and I won't be supporting you in it."

"Do you really think this is your decision?"

"Caleb." She sounded like she was scolding an exasperating child. "We are to be married. We need to be in unity over things."

"Really? So from now on, every time you don't like something I do, I have to bow to your will to be in unity with you? Is that how you think marriage works?" His tone carried his anger, and he had no wish to moderate it.

Kyla stepped back and tears welled in her eyes. "Well, if you can honestly say you think this is something that God wants you to do, then who am I to stand in your way?"

Caleb stepped around her and walked out of the locker room. He couldn't believe she'd brought God into it to manipulate the situation. The whole argument was stupid, and he was furious.

"Caleb, hey."

His eyes adjusted as he stepped into the sunshine and saw Sasha in her wheelchair. Alanah was pushing her. This was so not the time, but he dug deep and found a smile.

"Great game today," Sasha said. "How did he rate?" She turned her head to ask Alanah.

Alanah grinned. "He played well."

"But?" Caleb could hear a "but" and wanted to know why.

"I have to take the context into consideration," Alanah said. "Aussie rules obviously isn't played on a professional level here. This was just an exhibition match, right?"

"We have four teams in the district and play a number of games to make a season." He sounded defensive again.

"Well, it was fun to watch, and you did play well," Alanah said.

"Not good enough to play professionally?" Sasha grinned at her.

"Yeah, right." Caleb laughed. "They don't draft old players like me professionally to start with."

Alanah laughed and nodded. "For an old fella, you played really well. Good job."

Caleb forced a smile. Old fella? He was the same age as both of them, twenty-nine. He wasn't quite ready to be put out to pasture yet.

"Don't get all grumpy," Sasha said.

"Sorry I called you an old fella," Alanah said. "Most AFL players are retiring in their early thirties. The game is hard on the body."

Suddenly he could feel every bump and bruise from the day's game. Perhaps he was getting old. Still, he wasn't going to give up playing just because Kyla demanded it.

"Are you coming home now, or shall we go out for a celebratory pizza?" Sasha asked.

"Perhaps Kyla could come as well." Alanah passed a look to Sasha as she spoke, and Caleb didn't miss it. What was going on there?

"I'd love to come." Kyla. She'd approached quietly from behind, and he hadn't been aware she was standing there.

"Actually, why don't you girls go out and have pizza. I think I'd like to go home and have a soak in the tub. This will give you all a chance to get to know each other better."

Caleb watched the dynamic that silently spun around the circle. Sasha had just had her plans foiled, Kyla was looking for a way to get out of it, and Alanah … He couldn't read her expression. It seemed like happy acceptance. Whatever. He was tired from the strenuous game, and he didn't feel like pandering to Kyla's recently revealed insecurities. And goodness knows what Sasha had in mind. He didn't think she liked Kyla anyway. Too bad for her.

"I'll see you tomorrow at church." He shouldered his sports bag and headed towards his car. Let them sort it out.

"Sasha, I think your dislike of Kyla is kinda obvious." Alanah helped her friend get into the front seat of Marianne's car. "You're being quite rude to her, and that isn't really fair to Caleb."

Sasha ignored her and snapped her seatbelt into place.

"Sasha?" Alanah glared at her through the still-open passenger door.

"I'm tired too, Alanah. This is my first day out of hospital. It's best I get home and rest."

Marianne finished loading some Tupperware containers into the boot of the car and went around to the driver's side— which confused Alanah, because she was used to that side being the front passenger side. Big breath. Still trying to get used to everything being backwards when it came to road rules and left-hand drive.

"What are you girls talking about?" Marianne asked.

"Nothing," Sasha replied. "It's been a big day and I need to take some more pain meds."

"I told you it would be too much for you to come straight out of hospital," Marianne said.

Alanah settled herself in the back seat behind Marianne. She wasn't going to get into this. Sasha probably should have gone straight home to rest, but she'd insisted on coming.

"Who were you being rude to?" Obviously, Marianne's hearing was sharper than Alanah had thought.

"I wasn't rude. It's a legitimate excuse to want to go home."

"But you'd just invited everyone out for pizza." Alanah couldn't help but point out the obvious.

"I didn't invite Kyla."

"No, but I did, and she seemed keen to come."

"She wasn't keen once she knew Caleb wasn't going to come. She was glad I'd made the excuse."

"Perhaps, but it still seemed rude."

"Sasha." Marianne's firm mother tone was evident. "You might not like Kyla yet, but she is Caleb's choice of life partner, and it's going to be fairly miserable for you as his twin, if you insist on maintaining this intolerance."

Sasha mumbled something that Alanah couldn't make out, but Alanah agreed with Marianne. If Caleb loved Kyla, then Sasha was going to have to learn to love her too.

I'm going to have to love her as well.

A bucket of something sour turned in Alanah's stomach. She wished she could show her disappointment like Sasha did. This was going to be harder than she thought—weeks of being together with Caleb, while his focus and affection was directed towards someone other than her. She couldn't wait to get back to the house and get into bed. Thank goodness she still had lingering jetlag as an excuse to disappear under the covers.

CHAPTER SIX

The second Sunday had flown past in a whirl. Alanah had gone to church with James and Marianne while Sasha stayed home. She wasn't well enough and shouldn't have gone to the Anzac Day game. The rest of the Kennedy clan had found their own way to church. Lucy, Matthew, and Mia were all in their twenties and obviously had social lives of their own.

The senior Kennedys introduced Alanah to a load of people, but she only remembered the Australians. Jason Wainscott was nice, even if they did trade insults about each other's states. Alex Sinclair seemed like a good bloke, and a great musician. Alanah loved hearing the church worship band. Her small church back in South Australia didn't have the luxury of a small band to support the worship time. They were lucky to have an older lady play the piano, and the occasional accompaniment from a twelve stringed guitar. Still, it wasn't the quality of music that made worship a precious time.

By Monday morning, Alanah was ready to set out for the orientation week at Trinity Lakes Summer Camp.

"I better not come today," Sasha said. "I'm not feeling as well as I'd hoped. All the pain meds are making me dopey."

"I thought you were always dopey," Caleb said, stuffing a slice of vegemite toast in his mouth.

Alanah smiled but refrained from taking sides when it came to Sasha and Caleb.

"Will you take Alanah with you when you go?" Sasha said.

She was ignoring her brother's teasing. That was strange. Did she have ulterior motives?

"Sure. I have to swing by and pick up Kyla as well, but there's plenty of room."

Alanah watched Sasha's face fall. Her plans had been foiled again, and she didn't try to hide it. Caleb didn't rise to the bait. He was good at pretending.

Alanah had repacked a smaller bag for camp, just her outdoor and sports gear. There was no need to bring her Sunday best or clothes she'd brought for her tour north once summer camp was over.

"Shall I put my gear in your ute?"

Everyone in the kitchen laughed. Language difference strikes again.

"I haven't heard that term in …"

"Eleven years," Caleb finished off his mother's comment. "It's a truck, Alanah."

Truck. She knew that in theory, of course, but truck brought visions of a large load-carrying vehicle. Dad and Mitch had a couple of trucks to cart grain to the silos and move stock long distances. What Caleb drove was a ute. But when in Rome …

"I love hearing you talk, Alanah," Marianne said. "We loved those five years in the Australian bush."

"Good times," Matt said. "Do you know how long it took me to get rid of my Aussie accent when we got back to Trinity Lakes? Some of my mates still call me Dundee."

"You're not even Australian," Alanah said to Sasha's younger brother.

"Tell me about it. When I was at school in Australia, they

called me Yank, and when I got back, they said I sounded like an Australian. I'm a lost individual."

Alanah laughed. "You don't sound Australian, believe me. And by the way, my brother, Mitch, said to say g'day."

"Huh. Yeah." Matt looked thoughtful. "Mitch always called me "Yank" when we were at school."

"Yeah, he told me. Political correctness isn't his strong suit," Alanah said.

"Those five years in your country left an impact on all of us," James said as he put his breakfast dishes in the dishwasher. "We're American, but there's a space in our hearts that will always be Aussie."

"I hope you all come back and visit Down Under sometime," Alanah said.

"Let's go and get this summer camp orientation done first," Caleb said, putting his coffee cup in the sink. "Are you ready?"

Was she ready? To be with Caleb for two weeks? No. Not even. This was going to be horrible in so many different ways. The adventure of being at a real American summer camp was one thing, but watching Caleb and Kyla exchange affection was nothing short of drip torture.

———

THIS WAS AWKWARD. There was plenty of room for the camping luggage and sleeping bags in the back of Caleb's truck. Having Alanah sitting in the front seat next to him felt—great. It should not feel great. It should feel like nothing. And now they were approaching Kyla's house. She was going to throw a fit when she saw Alanah.

"Did Kyla know I was coming with you?"

Caleb saw the scowl on Kyla's face as they approached. It wasn't hard to read what was going through her mind.

50

"Don't worry about it," he said. "It's only logical to go together."

Alanah didn't say anything, but the moment he pulled to a stop, she scrambled out of the truck as if it was on fire.

"Thanks for letting me catch a ride with you," Alanah said to Kyla.

Kyla didn't answer. She was upset. He should be pleased that he was so attuned to her that he could read her mind. But now they were engaged, she was behaving like she owned him. He didn't like it. He'd have to talk to her about it when they were next alone.

"Are you looking forward to summer camp?" Alanah asked.

She was apparently anxious and trying to break the tension with Kyla. Funny. Caleb was equally attuned to Alanah. This was awkward to the max. He should have insisted Sasha organize for someone else to take Alanah.

"I've been to summer camp plenty of times," Kyla said. "It's nothing special."

"I thought you liked being part of the team, mentoring kids?" Caleb was not happy with Kyla's attitude and wasn't going to make it easy for her.

Alanah stood back, allowing Kyla to get in the front of the truck and slide across. Kyla gave him a steely glare. Caleb opened his eyes wider at her as if to ask a question. Why was she being so cold and nasty?

Alanah. That was obvious.

"This is the trip of a lifetime for me," Alanah said as she squeezed in and pulled the passenger door closed. "I'm so excited. Thanks for letting me be part of it."

She was trying to ignore Kyla's cold shoulder. Caleb's heart swelled with appreciation for her. Alanah was such a lovely person. It was time for him to ignore Kyla's insecurity and put Alanah at ease. It wasn't her fault that Kyla was jealous of her.

51

"Mind if we listen to some music while we drive?" He pressed the FM button, and a bright song filled the cabin.

"I love this song," Alanah said.

"Me too." Caleb was quick to respond. Kyla didn't say anything. This was going to be a long drive.

———

THIS WAS like *The Parent Trap*. Small log cabins were scattered around the campsite, a large meeting room, also made of logs, was obviously the activities hall. The kitchen and dining room situated near the meeting hall, was made of bricks. There were trees all over the area—pine, fir, and oak. It all appeared very American. Wow. She was finally here.

"Welcome to Camp Trinity." A smiling forty-something woman of Asian appearance greeted them with a local accent. She wore a fishing hat, khaki shorts, hiking boots, and a brightly colored t-shirt with Camp Trinity in multi-colored font, and carried a clipboard. "You must be Sasha's friend from Australia."

Alanah nodded.

"I've put you and Kyla in the same cabin as Sasha. Is Sasha still coming?" The woman glanced behind them as if expecting Sasha to materialize.

"She'll hopefully be all right to be here next week when the campers arrive," Caleb said.

"Her leg is still giving her a lot of pain," Alanah added. "She wanted to come, but it was a bad break and she had surgery only a week ago."

"I'll give her a call," the woman said. "I'm Caitlyn." She stuck out her hand for Alanah to shake. She was everything in friendliness that Kyla wasn't. But perhaps that wasn't fair. Kyla felt threatened by the arrival of an old friend. She didn't know the relationship between Alanah and Caleb was never going to go anywhere.

Kyla had already walked past Caitlyn and was heading towards a cabin. She really was being rude.

"You're in cabin seven." Caitlyn handed Alanah a key. "Settle yourself in and meet back in the meeting hall in half an hour."

"Thanks, Caitlyn. It's nice to meet you."

Caitlyn nodded.

Alanah walked across the compound following Kyla. She assumed she must know where cabin seven was, but when she got to the cabin Kyla had entered, it was cabin three. The name list pinned to the cabin showed it was one of the guys' cabins. This was Caleb's digs. Alanah sighed and stepped back down from the porch.

"Over that way." Caitlyn shouted and pointed to the opposite side of the grounds.

"Thanks." Alanah pasted a huge smile on her face. She was going to enjoy this experience. Kyla would get over it soon and realize she was behaving badly for no reason.

Alanah stepped onto the wooden porch of another cabin and found her name written on a card tacked to the wall beside the door. Kyla Ferguson, Sasha Kennedy, Alanah Walker, and the name of another girl. Belinda Gowen. Thank goodness it wasn't just going to be her and Kyla for the orientation week. Alanah opened the wooden fly-screen door and stepped inside.

"All right?" A woman in her early twenties, sitting on a made-up bunk with a journal in hand, smiled at Alanah. Her accent was decidedly British.

"Hi." Alanah smiled back. "I'm Alanah."

"From Australia. They told me we internationals would be together. My next adventure will be to the outback."

Alanah smiled. Everyone thought the outback was a wonderful place. It probably was, but there was so much else in Australia that was worth seeing, after you'd wandered about the red desert for a bit.

"I haven't met Sasha or Kyla yet." Belinda closed her journal, obviously ready for a chat. "They're both American, I think.

"Sasha is my best friend from high school," Alanah said.

"She's Australian?"

Alanah laughed. "No. Her family lived in Australia for five years during our high school years, and we were best friends before they returned here to Trinity Lakes."

"Did she come with you?" Belinda peered out the door as if expecting to see Sasha coming.

"Hopefully she'll be here next week when the campers arrive, but she's currently recovering from surgery for a bad break in her femur."

"Oh, wow. That's awful. I hope she'll be okay."

"Me too. We've planned a sightseeing trip after the summer camp. She's getting married in October, and I've never been to North America, so we've been looking forward to this. I'll be gutted if she can't come."

"I'm planning some tours as well. How many weeks of camp will you be doing?"

"I've only registered for three, including the orientation week."

"I've put my name down for six," Belinda said. "Shame. We could have travelled together if Sasha ends up not being able to make it."

It was nice of Belinda to suggest it, but Alanah balked at the idea. She'd come to spend time with Sasha before her wedding. They had spent months planning where they would go, booking accommodation and tours. It wouldn't be the same if she had to share the experience with a stranger.

Alanah pushed the worry about Sasha and their travel plans to one side while she made up a bunk and put some things in the bedside cabinet.

"You ready?" Belinda asked. "Not sure where Kyla Ferguson is. Maybe she won't be coming either."

"No, she's here. We came together." Alanah didn't feel like going into all the detail surrounding Kyla. Belinda would meet her soon enough. "Let's go to the meeting hall and find out what happens next."

The day had lost a bit of its sparkle. Sasha wasn't here. Kyla was here, lugging a semi-trailer load of attitude behind her wherever she went. That Caleb was here instead of Sasha might have added some joy, if it wasn't for the negative energy that came like a tractor beam in her direction if she so much as smiled in his direction. She hoped she'd be allocated a team who didn't emit aggression all the time.

Caitlyn and her husband, George, ran the introductory session. They were enthusiastic as they outlined what orientation week would look like. As camp leaders in training, they had to learn all the ins and outs of activities, safety procedures, and complete a first aid refresher course, but they also got to have a week of fun in the sun. So far so good. What could possibly go wrong?

"You'll all form teams this week, and those leaders will work together next week." George clicked through to the next slide on his PowerPoint presentation. "Each team will have a male and a female leader, and we've also made sure that our five international leaders are teamed with someone from the local area."

The team names flashed on the screen. Alanah was paired with Caleb, and they would work with Belinda and another guy —Ryan—who must be local. A stab of worry shot through her. She didn't have to study Kyla to know she'd be furious.

"You all have name tags, so you should be able to find the three people who will make up your training team for the week," Caitlyn said from the front of the room. "For the next half hour, we'd like you to sit in your teams and get to know each other. Then we'll set out for the first round of activities."

Alanah moved to the table where Belinda sat. She wasn't

going to pursue Caleb in any way. He and Ryan could come to them. But he didn't come. Another young man came and sat down with them. "Hi. I'm Ryan. I'm from Walla Walla."

Belinda laughed. "Walla Walla?"

"A town so nice they named it twice." Ryan smiled at them.

"Is that a saying that goes with the town?" Alanah asked.

"Sure." Ryan had a charming smile

"We have a town in Australia called Wagga Wagga."

Belinda laughed again. "Brilliant. I love it."

"Anyway, I'm Alanah, from ..."

"Australia?" Ryan asked.

"Booleroo Whim, to be precise, since we're sharing strange town names."

"I'm from Portishead in the UK," Belinda said. "Not far from Bristol."

"Where's Caleb Kennedy?" Ryan asked. "I haven't met him before."

Alanah glanced over to where Caleb and Kyla were in deep discussion with Caitlyn and George. She didn't have to be a mind reader to know what was going on there. She wasn't sure whether her stomach twisted with relief or disappointment.

———

"I'D PREFER it if Caleb and I worked together." Kyla had fronted up to the camp directors as if she owned the franchise.

This was embarrassing. Who did she think she was, making demands like this, and for what reason?

"I'm sorry, Kyla, but we deliberately put you and Caleb in separate teams because you're engaged." Caitlyn didn't appear sorry. She looked like she'd made her decision.

"That's the very reason we should be in the same team."

Caleb felt the strength of Kyla's personality and the depth of her fury and was repelled by both. He hadn't seen this side of Kyla before, and it was both unnerving and distressing.

"Once we have campers here, each leader needs to have full focus on the young people in their charge. There will be no opportunity for couples to share time together. In fact, that could be a dangerous distraction."

"Then don't put him in a team with that Australian girl."

"Kyla!" Caleb couldn't believe how rude she was being to Caitlyn. She was pushing the limits now.

She swung her eyes to hold him in a glare, sparks of fury leaping in his direction.

"I apologize," Caleb turned back to the camp leaders. "Just give us a few moments, and we'll sort this out."

George was uncomfortable, evidenced by the way he worried his nametag lanyard, but Caitlyn was five feet two inches of firm authority. She would not be easily swayed.

"Two seconds." He held up two fingers in their direction before turning towards his fiancée. "You can't be serious." Caleb didn't hide his annoyance, though he kept his volume down.

"I just want us to work together, Caleb. I can't see what the problem is."

"George and Caitlyn have already arranged the team leaders, as they said."

"It won't make any difference. Miles Duran, whoever he is, can most certainly show Alanah how things work in the US."

"Except Miles Duran is from New Zealand. He's an international leader and needs a local. Besides, I don't want to work with you while we're trying to monitor the activities."

"I would have thought …"

"No, Kyla. We will work in the teams as they've arranged, and I'd appreciate it if you didn't make any more fuss."

Caleb turned from her and nodded to the camp directors. "We'll be fine as you've arranged it," he said, then moved over to the table where Alanah sat with two other people.

By all appearances, Ryan Kozlanski had the two girls eating out of his hand. Before he even sat down, the two ladies burst out laughing. The way Alanah's face lit with animated joy and excitement as she joked with Ryan released a shaft of jealousy.

He had to stop right now. This was all for the better. He had to remain professional if he and Kyla were ever going to get over this hurdle in their relationship.

He didn't even spare Kyla a second glance. She'd figure it out on her own throughout the week. She had absolutely nothing to worry about—and neither did he. Alanah was well and truly over the teenage crush they used to share and could well be on the way to developing a new interest.

CHAPTER SEVEN

"So, Ryan's cute," Sasha said, the moment Alanah settled into her bunk on the first night of real camp a week later.

"You're engaged to be married, Sash," Alanah replied. She was so not up for a teenage girl-like discussion about boys. She'd already been around the campers' cabins twice, making sure the eighth and ninth grader girls were in their beds, and that there were no hormonal fourteen-year-old boys lurking around, waiting for an opportunity to sneak off in the darkness.

"How's your leg?" Belinda asked in the dim light.

"If it weren't for the pain meds, I'd be in a heap on the floor crying," Sasha said.

"Make sure you don't get addicted."

Thanks for the advice, Belinda.

Alanah was feeling out of sorts. She was still working with Caleb, and they had handled their group of teens well through all the introductory group activities. But she felt guilty. Kyla and her team were never far away from direct line of sight, and Alanah felt as if her every action was being scrutinized. It was taking all the fun out of her experience.

"Is Kyla doing a final check round the cabins?" Belinda asked. Goodness, she was persistent.

"Kyla is …" Running off into the darkness with Caleb. Such a bad example, but she wasn't her mother. "She's just catching up with her fiancé," Alanah eventually said.

"Really? Who's she engaged to?"

"My brother." There was no mistaking the lack of enthusiasm in Sasha's tone, but Alanah was used to that.

"Which one is your brother?" Belinda asked.

"Caleb. My co-team leader."

"You're kidding?" Belinda sounded just like the teenage girls they'd tucked safely into bed. "I thought he was …"

Was what? Alanah resisted the urge to ask. Sasha didn't have the same scruples.

"Was what?"

"Well, the way Alanah and he get on together, I thought that something might have been … you know … perhaps…"

"I'm only in the country for a short time." Did she sound snappy? Too bad. "I have no intention of forming a summer romance."

Sasha sniffed a suppressed giggle. Honestly. It must be the camping in dormitories that turned them into overgrown high-schoolers.

"I wouldn't mind a bit of flirting," Belinda said. "Ryan's nice, but his attention seems to be fixed on you as well."

Sasha snorted this time.

"Cut it out, Sash. Belinda, you should know, Sasha is not in favor of her brother's engagement."

"No kidding," Belinda said.

"And you might as well know, he and Alanah had a summer romance a few years ago." Thanks, Sasha. Belinda did not need to know they had history.

"Looks like something new might emerge."

"Cut it out. Both of you." Alanah did snap this time. "That

romance was *eleven* years ago and snuffed out pretty quickly when we discovered neither of us wanted to shift continents. And, in case you've forgotten, we are here as mature adults, guiding and mentoring impressionable teens towards healthy life and relationships. Giggling over boys is silly and not helping."

Sasha laughed. "You keep telling yourself that."

"I mean it, Sasha. You're not helping."

"I'm sorry, Alanah. I didn't mean to cause trouble." At least Belinda sounded repentant.

"Apology accepted. Just don't mention this in front of Kyla, or there will be trouble. She already feels insecure about Caleb."

"Well she shouldn't. Not if it's a real engagement," Sasha said.

"Of course it's real. Stop talking nonsense." Alanah was actually relieved when the cabin door opened, and she saw Kyla enter by the light of her mobile phone.

"What's real?" Kyla asked as she came to her bunk.

"The pain in my leg," Sasha said. Well at least she was quick enough to avert that possible clash.

"Did you see any teenagers out of bed?" Alanah asked. Was she the only one who cared enough to be diligent?

"Not that I noticed."

"Did you pop your head in each cabin?"

"I wouldn't want to wake them," Kyla said.

Alanah threw her cover off and her legs over the side of the bunk.

"Where're you going?" Belinda asked.

"To make sure they are asleep and safe." And to escape the silly discussion that had been going on.

"They'll be fine," Kyla said.

"I'll sleep better making sure." She left the cabin with her mobile phone in hand.

She wasn't ten meters from the cabin steps when she heard

the door open. It obviously wasn't Sasha, as she took forever to get about in her wheelchair. Belinda?

"I thought I'd best check with you." Kyla. What? Was she afraid Alanah was going to sneak out to meet Caleb or something? Honestly, her insecurity was out of control.

"You know there's nothing between Caleb and me, don't you?" Maybe it was time to clear the air.

"You seem fairly friendly."

"We *are* friends. Have been since we started high school. But I have no intention of stealing him from you, Kyla. He's a man of integrity. He wouldn't have asked you to marry him if he didn't want to follow it through. You doubting him doesn't show much faith in his character."

Kyla didn't say anything but kept following Alanah on her rounds of the girls' cabins. Every time they stepped onto a porch, there was a distinct sound of shushing. Obviously, the real teenagers were as involved with nighttime chat sessions as the leaders. Alanah opened each door.

"It's past midnight, girls. You'll need to get some sleep if you're going to enjoy the outdoor activities tomorrow."

Giggling. "She sounds like she's Australian, like Liam Hemsworth," someone whispered.

Just like Liam Hemsworth—or not.

"Girls." Alanah used the stern tone she employed with her Sunday School class. "Sleep."

She repeated the routine four times.

"You sound quite strict," Kyla said as they approached their own cabin.

"I want to sleep. I'm ruined."

"Me too."

At least that much they could agree on. Finally.

———

THE OCEAN BETWEEN US

AT AROUND TWO in the morning Alanah decided to let her worry go. She couldn't be stressing over errant teenagers all night and hope to be alert tomorrow. Besides, she wasn't the only leader on site who was on call to respond to an incident.

The sound of the brass bell, conveniently strung on an A-frame near the kitchen, intruded into Alanah's deep sleep. It couldn't be six o'clock already. Four hours was not long enough. Though she was tempted to pull the cover over her head and ignore the signal to rise, she knew it was her responsibility to get all the campers upright and conscious, ready for devotion time in half an hour.

"This is your moment to shine," Alanah grumbled at Sasha. "I hope you've got something sorted."

"Don't worry about me," Sasha replied. She had risen earlier and had emerged from the bathroom shining and sweet-smelling, despite her heavy cast. Alanah glanced at her watch and decided to reserve her shower for after the all-day activities in the sun. It might be good to dunk her head under the tap though, to help kick her brain into gear.

"Do you need a hand getting to the meeting area?" Belinda asked. She was a caring person.

"Thanks, Belinda. Are you ready to go now? I need to set up and get ready for devotions."

Belinda carried Sasha's Bible and notebook, following her as she hobbled to the wheelchair, parked on the ground beside the porch. Alanah felt a pang. She should have been the one helping her best friend. Instead, she was fighting the late-night cotton-wool brain and hoping not to have another intense moment with Kyla.

Sasha was brilliant in her presentation. She knew how to engage the young people with interaction, allowing them input in the discussion, rather than just preaching at them. There was no doubt that this current generation of teens had many areas of angst, and with small prompts, questions and animated discussion flowed. Alanah was impressed and moved when a number of young people requested personal prayer.

Breakfast was unusually hearty for a camp. Eggs and bacon, pancakes, and syrup. Excellent, until she saw that most people put syrup on their bacon. Why? There was no accounting for American taste. Alanah kept her pancake and syrup carefully separate from her eggs and bacon. Weird.

"How did you sleep?" Caleb gathered the milk crate containing the fruit and clipboard they would need as they set out to all of their activities.

"Fine, after a number of reconnaissance rounds in the dark." Alanah shouldered the emergency first aid backpack that would follow them all the while outdoors.

"Reconnaissance? What were you doing outside in the dark?"

"Making sure there were no straying kids, and that they all went to sleep."

Caleb laughed. "What time did you give up?"

Alanah frowned. "What makes you think I gave up?"

"Those kids can go all night. It's first night excitement. They're unlikely to go to sleep early, if at all."

Alanah glanced around at the youth still in the dining room on clean up duty. Definite signs of dark circles under the eyes, but they didn't seem to be flagging for energy.

"Do you think they'll go to sleep earlier tonight?" she asked.

"Maybe. Though I wouldn't pace the perimeter all night. One or two rounds to make sure they're all tucked in usually does it."

"You've done summer camp before?"

"A couple of times, but it was a few years ago."

"Did you ever go to summer camp as a teen?"

"I was in Australia with you when I was a teen, remember? We had a few school trips, and those couple of youth camps we attended. Of course, they were in the middle of winter. But similar, I guess."

Alanah followed Caleb out the door and down to the ropes course. Their group's first activity for the day—tree-top rope climbing. She cast her mind back to the school camps she'd been on. A trip to the Grampians in Victoria. A bit of bush walking, then the Gold Rush Museum in Ballarat. That was fascinating. But most of her trips had been of an educational nature, and she had never actually done rope climbing before. As kids, they'd swung out on a homemade flying fox—a pulley strung on a long cable between two trees—any number of times before the local council had decided it didn't meet the necessary health and safety standards. But last week, on orientation, she'd loved being hooked to a zip line and moving about the treetops and high wires.

It wasn't quite as much fun keeping energetic teens within the bounds of safety and watching them have all the fun roaming the treetops while her feet never left the ground.

"Are you going to go up again?" Caleb asked.

"I guess we'd best stay put and make sure the little ducks are safe."

"Anton and I can keep that sorted down here. Have another go."

Anton, the resident climbing expert nodded. "I've got it from here."

Alanah studied Caleb. It had been exciting when she'd tried it last week. "Are you sure?"

"Go." Caleb handed her a harness and after Anton checked it, she was up high, mingling with the younger campers.

"Watch your feet, Alanah," one helpful camper pointed out. "Don't want to have you hanging upside down and having to rescue you."

"Ha. Mind your own feet. I'll be perfectly all right."

The overconfident boy beamed at her. Was that a teenage crush? Oh, to be fifteen again.

But her own boasting wasn't as grounded as it should have been. She was one of the last ones to descend, and when she did, her foot slipped, and she dangled out away from the tree.

"Are you all right?" Caleb called. If she hadn't let out a panicked shriek, she could have coiled in her pride and got herself back to ground without the well-intentioned call to rescue coming from below.

"Here, take my hand." The fifteen-year-old boy who'd flirted with her before was on the platform and reached out to assist her. This was embarrassing. She resisted taking his hand and tried to swing herself in a couple of times, but she had to grab something, and his hand was the only thing available.

"I'll rescue you." The cheesy grin was priceless, matched with the skinny physique and barely formed muscles.

"You better not fall," Alanah said as she swiped to grab his hand.

"You okay?" Caleb from below. Again. Mature man out of reach. Teenage boy in shining armor. Oh, the irony.

Alanah grasped the junior hero's hand. The momentum from her weight wanted to swing back and he was in danger of toppling from the platform to join her dangling in mid-air. She noted the determination on his face as he dug deep and engaged every muscle fiber he owned. For a moment she thought he'd lose grip, but he didn't, and he eventually hauled her back. She sensed they were both a bit wobbly when she finally got both feet on the small wooden platform.

"See, I saved you." He still had hold of her hand, and his smile was from ear to ear. Bless him.

"Thank you. I appreciate your effort, Max." From this close vantage, she was able to read the sticker with his name on it. The stickers would probably end up scrunched in the dirt by the end of the day but they were helpful right now for learning names.

"Will you take a selfie with me? I want to post it to my Snapchat."

Really? Teenaged boys did Snapchat?

"Sure. Once we're back on terra firma."

Max stood back while Alanah descended first. The rest of the group were standing about, necks craned upward.

"Sure you're all right?" Caleb asked as Anton unclicked the zip line.

"Nothing like a little adventure, right?" Alanah smiled at him.

With that, Max sidled right next to her, his smart phone in hand.

"I'm surprised you want to post on Snapchat," Alanah said to the boy. "Do you post often?"

"Nah. Not really."

She raised her eyebrows in a question.

"It's just you look like that Australian actress."

"Which one?" Caleb asked. "Nicole Kidman?"

"Who?" Max frowned.

Not Nicole. That was good. She didn't think she looked like Nicole.

"Cate Blanchett?" Caleb offered.

More puzzled expressions.

"No, the one who played Jane in the last Tarzan movie."

"Margot Robbie. Oh. Right." Did she look like Margot? She didn't think so, but she'd take it.

"And she's Australian, like you."

There was no getting past him. She allowed him to put his arm around her and tilt his head closer while he held the phone out at arm's length.

What was that expression on Caleb's face?

Max took his shot and stepped away to where their other team members were eating fruit and drinking water.

"What's the matter?" Alanah asked Caleb.

"He's got a crush on you."

"Really? I hadn't noticed." She had a black belt in sarcasm.

Caleb screwed up his mouth.

"It will be fine," Alanah said. "Didn't you ever have a crush when you were fifteen?"

"Yeah."

"And you got over it, didn't you?"

"No." Caleb said. He didn't say anything else but continued putting harnesses in the tubs.

Whatever.

CHAPTER EIGHT

He shouldn't be jealous of a fifteen year old. Wait, he shouldn't be jealous over Alanah at all. When Kyla came to Caleb at lunch time and kissed him, guilt attacked him from the side. He was engaged to Kyla, yet he hadn't thought about her the whole morning. He'd been too busy watching Max, the underage ladies' man, gloating over how he'd rescued Alanah. She hadn't needed rescuing. She was quite capable of righting herself safely and unassisted. Yet she'd accepted the boy's help, and he'd nearly burst into flames. That made two of them—Max from pride, and Caleb from an emotion he shouldn't be feeling. He had to get a grip.

The after-lunch activity for their group was canoeing. There was no way Caleb would allow Max to be in Alanah's canoe.

As with all the activities, there was a resident expert, Hannah Gilbertson from the rowing club, who gave the campers a short lecture on water safety and how to manage the paddle. Caleb buzzed around helping the kids get their life jackets properly secured.

It didn't take long before all the young people in his group were set in pairs, and some had already pushed out into the

lake. Caleb pushed his canoe out with Max as his paddling partner. The boy had hung around until the end, probably hoping to
get into Alanah's canoe, so Caleb deftly maneuvered Max to be
in his boat.

It was magnificent weather to be out on the water. Bucket
hats and sunscreen smeared on faces, the happy laughter of
young people having a good time trying to coordinate paddling
together in such a way that they could steer their boats around
the lake.

Fifteen minutes into the exercise, Caleb noticed Alanah had
pulled her canoe alongside another boat with two girls in it.
There was an intense exchange going on.

"Max, let's paddle over to see if Alanah is okay." Like Max
would object. The boy was in love.

"Somethings wrong with Lian," Max said.

One of the girls in the other boat was holding on and crying,
as if in terror. As they approached, Alanah spoke to her in a
smooth and calming tone.

"It's going to be all right, Lian. Just take a deep breath."

"I can't." The panic-stricken girl sounded as if she was struggling to breathe. "Let me get out."

"We're in the middle of the lake, Lian. Just take a breath, and
we'll get you back to the shore as quickly as possible."

"No!" A sharp intake of breath, held.

Caleb managed to pull his canoe along on the other side of
Lian's. Max seemed to have a sixth sense for rescue, as he didn't
panic, and did all the right things to make it easy.

"See. Caleb and Max are here now." Alanah said. "It's going
to be all right."

"I might drown." Lian's fingers were holding the side of the
canoe in a white-knuckled grip. She'd lost her paddle, which
appeared to be floating atop the water several yards away.

"We won't let you drown." Caleb held the side of Lian's

canoe to keep it steady. "How about I get your oar, and we paddle back to the shore. See, it isn't far."

Instead of responding calmly to his suggestion Lian's short breaths sounded as if she were gasping for air. She had started trembling, and sweat broke out on her forehead. Caleb threw a glance in Alanah's direction. She shook her head ever so slightly. The message was plain. *Don't push her.* What should we do? He willed Alanah to hear his unspoken query.

"It's all right, Lian." Alanah's tone was smooth and reassuring, but Lian was still bunched tight with tension, her face still pale, and her breathing was still shallow.

"Let's do a big slow breath together," Alanah continued. "Ready. Slowly. In. Out."

Caleb found himself following the instruction, and a quick glance at Max and Lian's paddling companion saw they were also taking slow, deep breaths.

"Another one. You're doing great." Alanah's tone was so encouraging, and Caleb saw Lian's shoulders relax a couple of degrees. Still a long way to go.

After several minutes of soothing reassurance, Alanah went a step further.

"If Caleb gets your paddle, do you think you and Joanne could get back to shore?"

Though Joanne nodded, her eyes wide with worry, but obviously eager to resolve the tension, Lian balked, tensing again.

"It's okay." Caleb spoke this time. "I've got another plan."

Alanah cast him a hopeful glance.

"Finley?" He spoke to the boy in Alanah's canoe. "Do you think you could swap places with Lian, and you can row with Joanne?"

"Sure." The teen twisted to get into position.

"No. I can't. Stop!" Lian's waving hands and high-pitched tone said she was panicking again.

Everyone settled and looked to Caleb for another plan, anxiety drawn on each face.

"That's okay," he said quickly. "Don't worry. We'll think of something else."

Alanah gave him a wide-eyed look. He couldn't mistake the message—be careful.

"What if Alanah swaps with Joanne?"

The freckles on Lian's face stood out against her pale clammy skin. The fear in her eyes was not fake. She was terrified.

"Will that be all right?" Alanah asked. "I'll hop into your canoe, and I'll get us back to shore."

There was just the tiniest nod from Lian.

"Finley, you must hold Lian's canoe as steady as you can. Max and I will hold from this side." Caleb's instruction found a willing participant as Finley settled his paddle across the canoe and reached with both hands to hold the middle canoe steady.

Alanah brought her knees up into a crouch position preparing to stand.

"Carefully, now, Joanne. You stand up and we'll try to swap at the same time," Alanah said.

Joanne handed her paddle to Max and pushed herself up to a standing position at the same time as Alanah.

"No! Stop! You'll drown us all! Stop! Stop! Stop!" Lian's scream split the air just as Joanne stretched her foot over the edge of the canoe.

It all happened in an instant. The boys holding the canoes let go in confusion and everything became unstable. Joanne tried to correct and sit back down, but her foot caught on the edge of her canoe. She lost her balance, falling sideways and hitting her head on the edge of Alanah's canoe, before tumbling into the water. Had she knocked herself out? Caleb didn't stop to think but launched himself out of his canoe and into the water after Joanne.

He duck-dived into the murky lake water, swimming toward where he thought Joanne had gone under. It didn't take long to find her. The life vest brought her back to the surface, but unfortunately, she had a large gash above her right eyebrow, which was bleeding profusely. She wasn't in a panic but wasn't altogether compos mentis either.

"It's all right, Joanne. Just relax. I'll tow you back to the shore." Caleb urged Joanne to float on her back, while he cupped his hand under her chin, bringing her in using the life-saving sidestroke.

———

ALANAH WATCHED as Caleb disappeared under the water to rescue Joanne, then turned her attention back to Lian. She was in total meltdown, screaming and rocking the boat —literally.

"Move your boat away," Alanah shouted to Max. "I'll get in the boat with her, and you pull. Give me the paddle." She shouted this to Finley.

Alanah placed her left foot into the spot Joanna had vacated on the other canoe, which rocked. She needed to get both feet over and sit down and stabilize the boat. As she moved her right foot, Lian stood up and screamed.

"She's drowning," Lian shouted, her panic evident. "You have to save her. Don't sit down. Don't! She's drowning."

"Sit down, Lian." Alanah had lost her calm, soothing tone. Far from being able to calm her down, Alanah's presence seemed to be acting as a further trigger point. The situation had got out of control, and she needed to take charge. If she thought that Lian would suddenly see reason and sit calmly down, she was severely mistaken. She reached out to the panicked teenager. If only she could get her to sit down. But Lian thrashed about, still screaming.

"Settle!" Alanah yelled, the word in complete contrast to her tone.

The canoe tipped further, and no amount of trying to stabilize it made any difference. Arms winding in the air like a windmill, Alanah felt the boat go over. She wasn't worried about drowning. She'd completed her Royal Life Saving Bronze Star her final year of high school. Of course, being from the inland, it was done in the local swimming pool, with no waves, sand, or dangerous sea creatures. No sea creatures in this lake either, unless you counted Lian.

They were both in the water now.

Lian wasn't hard to find as her high-visibility life jacket was easily seen. Alanah swam across to her.

"Just relax, Lian. I can get you back to the shore easily if you just lie on your back."

Well, that was optimism right there. As if Lian was going to relax and trust anybody to get close to her. Alanah reached out to the thrashing Lian, but she grabbed hold of Alanah around the neck, and pulled both of them under. What was the maneuver she was supposed to use in this situation? It had been years since lifesaving training, and she'd never had occasion to use it. How strong could a panicked teenager be? If only she could dislodge her arms from around her neck, she could get them both back above water. This was crazy. Being underwater, Alanah couldn't even try to talk to Lian.

In fact, it was time to breathe, and Alanah couldn't get herself away from the panicking teen who was pulling her down. She couldn't drown. She was the holder of a Bronze Star from the Royal Life Saving Society, and she had a life vest on—a life vest that was struggling against the opposite force keeping her under.

Lian, stop!

No voice, no facial expression, no body language. Where was mental telepathy when you needed it?

She didn't believe it. It was as if all Lian's frantic prophecy had enabled the dismal outcome. Lian was going to drown. Alanah was going to drown.

And then, miraculously, Lian let go. Or had she succumbed? Alanah had just enough energy left to kick her way back to the surface, where she immediately gasped for air and coughed. It took a moment for her to stop worrying about herself and remember her responsibility. Lian? Where was Lian? Treading water, Alanah moved around, searching. There. What a relief. Caleb had Lian and was using the lifesaving sidestroke to bring her back to shore. Finley was helping Joanne, so that left only her—and Max.

"Are you okay?" Max was in the water next to her. There was an expression of concern on his face, but the last thing she needed was to be rescued by this would-be romantic hero.

"I'm fine, Max. Air and being able to breathe does wonders."

"Are you sure? Do you want me to …"

"I'm sure. We should perhaps try to rescue at least two of these canoes. You grab those floating paddles, and hand them to me in the canoe."

"Do you need help getting into the canoe?" He swam a stroke closer.

Not on your life. "I'll be fine. You get the paddles."

It was all very well to turn down a gallant offer for help, but hoisting oneself into an unstable canoe wearing heavy, water-logged clothes was harder than she'd thought. By the time she'd rolled over the side, she felt like a beached whale. It didn't seem to deter Romeo, however, as he swam over with the paddle within seconds.

"You okay?" he asked again. "Do you want me to …"

"You get in the other canoe and bring it back to shore. Thanks, Max."

He grinned like he'd won the favor of the high school beauty queen. What a laugh. He was easy to please, given she was soggy and bedraggled, and—knowing her luck—probably had pond slime clinging to her hair.

———

WHAT A DISASTER. To make matters worse, Caleb observed Kyla standing on the shore with worry written all over her face, her passel of teenagers straight from the archery field, milling about, some with bow and arrow in hand. Caleb felt a little like Robin Hood dragging himself ashore. Of course, Robin Hood didn't have a half-drowned teenager. Oh, for a dignified Morgan Freeman, bringing steady support on the beach, instead of an angsty fiancée.

"What happened?" Kyla's words had the demanding tone that was becoming all-too familiar, which annoyed Caleb. He wanted to make sure Alanah was all right, but he had Lian to tend to, who was breathing—thank goodness—and much more subdued. He ran a quick inspection out to the center of the lake. Most of their team had pulled up on shore and had formed a small crowd. Hannah was helping some anxious teens to stow their canoe safely.

Only Alanah and Max were still in the middle. That kid was too much. How did he always manage to be in the hero role?

"Caleb. What happened?" Kyla sounded impatient.

"Give me a couple of minutes, Kyla, please." He knew he sounded snappy, but there were forty-three things happening at once.

"I'm sorry, Caleb." Lian spoke. She sounded focused and sensible. That was good. "I'm sorry. I didn't mean to ..."

"It's okay," he said. "Do you usually panic around water?"

She shook her head, tears welling in her eyes. "I'm sorry." She was stuck on repeat. He could talk about this later. Right now, he was too fixated on what was going on out in the middle of the lake.

"You saved me," Lian said. "I would have drowned if you hadn't saved me."

Caleb resisted the urge to point out that there would have been no emergency at all if she had simply let them row her back to the shore when the panic hit.

"Hey, mate." Miles Duran, Kyla's assistant leader, spoke with a decidedly Kiwi accent. "You take your injured teens back to the meeting hall for attention. Kyla and I will round both teams up and take care of them for the rest of the session."

"Thanks, Miles. That would be great."

Kyla turned a shade of purple. It wasn't what she wanted, that much was obvious.

"Come on, Kyla. Let's take them all over to the grassed area and talk about what we'll do."

Thank heavens for Miles. The voice of reason whose e's sounded like i's and i's sounded like u's.

By the time Miles had cleared the shore of rubber-necked campers, Caleb was left with Lian, Finley, and Joanne. Max and Alanah were paddling two canoes back towards them side by side. The lurking green monster was the most stupid and inappropriate thing ever. He needed to get a grip. Get some perspective. Get some Tylenol.

"Joanne's head is still bleeding," Finley said. "Shall I take her to the meeting hall?"

"Just wait a couple of seconds. Alanah and I will take Joanne and Lian up together, then you and Max can join the others."

Separate Max from Alanah was first. Then he saw blood was still running down Joanne's face, and he cursed himself for a stupid fool. Where was the first aid kit?

CHAPTER NINE

"Alanah, Joanne looks like she needs stitches," Caitlyn said. "You and Caleb can take her to the medical center."

"Of course," Alanah said. A trip with Caleb. That was nice—and awkward.

"Caleb, you'll need her medical paperwork. It's in the office. I'll contact Lian's parents—they live in Trinity Lakes." Caitlyn led the way to the office. Apparently, Joanne's parents had taken the opportunity during summer camp to leave their kids and go on a short trip to Florida.

Five minutes later, Alanah tapped her fingers nervously on the car door handle. She had Joanne loaded in the back seat of Caitlyn's car, a sterile pad attached to her head with a firm bandage, ready for the trip into the Trinity Lakes Medical Center. This wasn't exactly how Alanah had planned to explore the amenities of the town. Finally, Caleb crossed from the office block, got into the driver's seat, and put his seatbelt on.

"That took forever," he said. "How are you feeling, Joanne?" He started the car, indicated, and pulled slowly onto the road.

When she didn't answer, Alanah twisted in her seat to see. "She's asleep. I hope that's not a bad sign." Alanah was well

THE OCEAN BETWEEN US

Caleb had only driven a hundred yards, so pulled over.

Alanah got out of the front passenger seat and opened the door to the back. Even as she climbed in, Joanne stirred.

"Are we there already?" Joanne asked.

Did she sound groggy?

"Another ten minutes or so." Caleb indicated and pulled back onto the road.

"Why did we stop?"

"We only just started, but you were asleep, and it's not good to let you sleep if you have concussion." Alanah smiled, hoping to be reassuring. "I'm sure you'll be all right, but we need to see if you need some help with that cut on your head."

"Do you think Lian will be all right?" Joanne asked. "She nearly drowned."

"She had a panic attack," Caleb said from the driver's seat.

"She's not usually like that," Joanne said. "I guess it must have been the accident."

"What accident?" Alanah asked.

"Her cousin died after a freak wave washed him from a fishing boat."

"Wow." Now Lian's reaction made sense.

"How long ago was the accident?" Caleb asked.

"Several months ago, I think. They were on a fishing trip when a storm hit. She was upset about it, but I didn't realize it had affected her so much."

Alanah fell quiet. The whole lake incident had thrown the campsite into chaos, and now she was in a car with Joanne ... and Caleb.

Kyla's jealousy was palpable. Alanah felt bad. Her friendship with Caleb was as strong as ever, but the edge of where they might have gone was also still present. Not that they would go anywhere—in a relationship sense—but Kyla didn't seem to believe Alanah when she'd tried to tell her, and now Kyla was obviously in a knot. The thing Kyla didn't realize was, the more she harangued Caleb, the more he withdrew. Alanah wished she could give her some relationship advice. The possessive thing was never going to work and could be Kyla's undoing.

"We're here." Thank you Captain Obvious. If the large-lettered sign saying Trinity Lakes Medical Center hadn't given it away, the large red emergency department sign probably would have given them a clue.

"Can you take Joanne into ER? I'll find a place to park the car."

Alanah nodded. It was as good a plan as any.

Joanne was not unsteady on her feet but complained of a headache. Hopefully that ache was due to the large gash on her forehead, and not to anything more sinister.

———

It was past seven by the time Alanah and Caleb got back into Caitlyn's car for the return trip to the campsite. It had been busy in the emergency room and taken some time before Joanne saw the doctor. They had applied a couple of butterfly stitches to the cut, and recommended she be watched for concussion for the next twenty-four hours. Joanne's parents had sent her grandparents to take responsibility for her, but they hadn't arrived until six thirty.

The doctor had quickly examined Alanah, then pronounced there was nothing to worry about. That wasn't a surprise. Alanah hadn't thought it necessary to come in the first place. Acting as Caleb's companion on the trip had already caused trouble with Kyla, and trying to pretend she didn't care about him was wearing thin.

"That was an eventful first day at summer camp." Alanah leaned back in the passenger seat.

"You managed to get in a tangle a couple of times."

What was that tone in Caleb's voice? She turned and frowned at him.

"What are you saying?"

"Max seemed to be on hand and happy to come to your aid."

"Caleb Kennedy, are you suggesting I orchestrated those mishaps?"

He had the good grace to look chagrined.

"If you must know, Max is a nice kid. And he did help me a couple of times."

"I know. I saw."

"And—your point?"

"He has a crush on you."

"I know. We discussed this already, remember?"

"Mmm."

"And while we're discussing our day, I have to ask. Why is Kyla so insecure about your relationship?"

Caleb didn't say anything.

"I'm no expert, but I'd say you could do a better job of reassuring her."

"I could reassure her all day. It wouldn't make any difference. She senses something."

Alanah wanted to ask what, but did she really want to know the answer?

"I'm not sure it's going to work."

"What?" Alanah turned to glare at him as he drove.

"Kyla and me."

"Caleb. You can't be so fickle with her feelings."

"Are you talking from experience?"

What was that hurt that stabbed her heart? She was well over that heartbreak, wasn't she?

"I felt bad about how we broke up," Caleb said.

"We didn't really break up." Were they really going to discuss this?

"It felt like a breakup to me."

"We were hardly going out together."

"Come on, Alanah. I was crazy about you. I thought you were crazy about me too."

She paused. Crazy hardly described it. More like long-term friendship she thought would never end—or wouldn't end until they had lived their lives together.

"So it didn't affect you?" Caleb asked as they drove through the winding roads back towards Camp Trinity.

"Of course it affected me. I was devastated."

"And yet ...?"

"We came to this last time we discussed it. I'm Australian. You're American. We're both attached to our family and country. It couldn't work. I reconciled to it years ago. Haven't you?"

This time Caleb didn't say anything. What did that silence mean?

"I hope you're not thinking of ending things with Kyla because of me."

The stony silence thickened from the drivers' side.

"Caleb. Don't sabotage a good thing with Kyla. You and I cannot work. You know that. Nothing has changed." Nothing. Alanah turned and studied his expression.

"Caleb?"

"I still feel strongly ..."

"About Kyla?"

No reply.

"You can't mean you still feel strongly about me. Caleb?"

"It is as it is. I can't do anything about it."

"It can't work. There's nothing to be gained by entertaining those thoughts."

"How do you feel?"

"About what?"

"About me."

"Caleb. Don't do this. Please."

"I just need to know."

"Why?"

"Because I do."

"Discussing this will undermine your relationship with Kyla. Then I'll return to Australia, and you'll be left with nothing."

This conversation was impossible, and all those feelings of the past were lined up at the gate, ready to break free. She couldn't. Could she?

"I'll let it go forever if you'll just be honest with me."

Who was he kidding?

"Alanah?"

"Caleb, I wish more than anything that it had worked out."

"So you … what? How did you feel about me? How do you feel about me now?"

"I love you, Caleb. Always have, but I'm doing my best to keep those feelings in the friend zone, as should you. You are engaged to be married. Kyla is freaking out about your past relationship with me, and you know …"

"I don't care about Kyla. Not like I care about you."

Alanah glared at him. She hoped he could see her in his peripheral vision. What a terrible thing to say.

"Don't look at me like that. I should never have proposed to her. We were good enough as friends, but the longer we dated, she kept hinting, and I didn't know how much I still cared …"

"Caleb. Stop! You can't be talking like this to me. It's wrong, and I don't like it."

He fell silent.

"Let's just get back to camp, and forget we ever spoke about it. Okay?"

He said nothing.

Alanah let out a frustrated sigh. If only he knew how close she was to letting herself go and throwing herself into his arms.

But she couldn't.

She wouldn't.

If she thought she was heartbroken eleven years ago, it would be a thousand times worse if she engaged her feelings this time and then left—because she would leave. Trinity Lakes was not her home, and never would be.

———

CALEB HAD to forget about having ever spoken about it. Sure. Easy. And so not going to happen. But Alanah was right. She was never going to leave Australia permanently.

But that didn't mean things with Kyla would work out. Fiancée or not, he didn't love her—not like he should, anyway. In fact, he was beginning to resent having to think about her. Who could think about Kyla when Alanah was sitting right next to him, so close that he could reach out and take her hand?

Two hands on the wheel, man.

It was wise both from a road safety point of view and so he could protect his heart. If only he could be angry and hurt with Alanah. Maybe that would have made it easier. But he couldn't. She was right. He was stupid for having brought it up. How was he going to last the rest of the two weeks at summer camp?

Perhaps Alanah was right. Perhaps he should just focus on Kyla, shower her with attention, and pretend no one else could ever take her place.

Pretend. What a great idea.

He didn't say anything else as they had arrived back at the campground. It was still light, and there were a number of kids engaged in the different free time activities around the site—tennis, basketball, table tennis. Dinner was obviously over, not that Caleb felt hungry anymore. The conversation with Alanah had stolen his appetite.

"Goodnight, Caleb." Alanah got out of the car and walked toward her cabin without a backward glance. It was never going to happen with her. He should get that in his head and deal with it.

As he clicked the key fob to lock the car he sensed, rather than saw, someone watching him from the veranda of the main meeting hall.

"You took a long time." Kyla.

Moment of decision. Allow the resentment to take charge and break it off, or change his attitude and reassure her of his dedication? Half-hearted dedication. Could it grow if he applied himself?

"What took so long?" That accusatory tone was there and provoked the simmering resentment.

"Let me give these keys back to Caitlyn, and then we can talk."

As he opened the door to the dining room, he saw there were still a few campers finishing off a hot chocolate.

"Everything okay?" Caitlyn greeted Caleb as he entered.

"The doctors patched Joanne's cut with butterfly stitches, and her grandparents came to get her. There is a slight chance of concussion, but they'll monitor her overnight. She may return to camp tomorrow or the day after if she feels confident."

"And Alanah?"

"She's fine. She didn't really need to come."

"It's usual practice to send two staff with a camper for any offsite medical treatment."

"Right."

"Anyway, I'm glad you're all okay. Are you good to help settle everyone for the night?"

"Sure." He held the keys out and dropped them in Caitlyn's hand. "Are there any late-night activities?"

"We'll have some time around the campfire for an hour or so, then we'll recommend everyone turn in. It's been a big day in the outdoors."

Caleb could have done without the campfire, but he was on this camp for a reason, so he determined to suck it up. He would find time to have it out with Kyla later.

"Is Alanah okay?" Sasha was sitting on a log near the bonfire with her guitar on her knee, ready to launch into song.

"She's fine. No need to panic."

"Where is she?"

"How should I know?"

"There's no need to be snappy."

Was he being snappy? Probably. Internal conflict will do that.

"She went to her cabin when we got back."

"Why? Did you have a fight with her?"

"Sasha. Honestly. Why would I have a fight with her?"

Sasha shrugged. "I thought you might have … you know…?"

"No, I don't know." He did, but there was no way he was going to admit that to his sister.

Caleb turned his focus to some of the kids he knew.

"How are Joanne and Lian?" Max asked.

"They're both all right now. Thanks for your help this afternoon."

Max grinned.

Caleb didn't linger. Max was probably a great kid, but it rankled how much he gushed over Alanah. And it shouldn't matter.

Sasha was a natural when it came to engaging teenagers. It wasn't long before she had them singing. She started with fun songs and got some confident campers to help her with some silly improvisation skits. By the time the evening had wound down, they had sung some worship songs. For a short while, Caleb breathed in the cool evening air and marveled at the magnificence of the starry night. With his eyes wide open, he stared at the heavens and remembered the summer nights he'd spent in Australia. Being near the outback, the sky had been darker and the stars more brilliant. There was no light pollution within fifty miles, which made the black velvet night sky sparkle with the jewelry of a million stars and the painted beauty of the Milky Way. The heavens declared the glory of the Lord, and Caleb loved it.

"Caleb?"

He fell with an emotional thud back to the present. Sasha had dismissed the campers, and most of them had gone. Kyla sat down next to him.

"Can we talk?" She rested her elbows on her knees.

He nodded.

"Are you going to be serious about our relationship, or are you going to chase after her?"

"Are you serious?" A fire lit in his chest. "Are you completely serious, Kyla? Do you know how much this possessive thing is annoying? I wish you'd cut it out."

Kyla recoiled, and Caleb felt a shard of regret. That was harsh—especially considering the conversation he'd had in the car on the way back from the medical center.

"I'm sorry, Kyla, but every time you're around, you're always making me feel guilty about my friendship with Alanah."

"Is there reason for you to feel guilty?"

"Do you want the truth?"

Kyla fixed a stare in his direction, as if she'd strapped on her emotional armor and was daring him to charge.

"I don't feel guilty about talking to Alanah, or laughing with her, or generally enjoying her company. She's my friend from way back ..."

"Come on, Caleb. I know you used to have a thing."

"A very short-lived thing that couldn't survive the Pacific Ocean between us." True but not the whole truth.

"But she's here now."

"Until Sasha's wedding. Then she'll go back to Australia. She is attached to her family and home. She won't stay here for me or for anyone else. You don't have to be jealous of her."

"What if she stayed? You'd take her back in a moment, wouldn't you?"

Caleb could almost feel his face turn to granite. What did she want from him?

"Wouldn't you?"

She wanted the truth, good, bad, or ugly. She wanted the truth. And she deserved the truth.

"I would. Alanah and I are like two halves of each other."

"Unlike you and me."

"Kyla, why are you forcing this? I proposed to you. I intend to marry you."

"Do you?"

"That's what the ring on your finger means, doesn't it?"

"I don't know, Caleb. You tell me."

"I'm tired and need to do the rounds of the boys' cabins. Can we talk about this another time?"

Kyla nodded. "Can you just answer one question?"

Caleb raised his eyebrows and tilted his chin in a signal to go ahead.

"Is there anything between us worth fighting for?"

Everything in Caleb screamed "No," but his voice contradicted him. "Of course. We're just tired. Let's talk about this at a more appropriate time."

———

ALANAH WASN'T SURPRISED—IN fact, she was relieved—when Caitlyn arranged a change of working partner. Caleb would now work with the British girl, Belinda, and Alanah was paired with Ryan Kozlanski from Walla Walla. Ryan was fun and good-looking. He flirted too, but in a much more subtle way than the fifteen-year-old Max.

Should she just join in the light-hearted flirting? It wasn't going to go anywhere. If she was going to emotionally engage with an American, she would have done that long ago. She had to stop thinking of Caleb. He'd obviously made the decision to focus on Kyla and asking to swap working partners was evidence of that. And so now, she was back to fending off silly questions from Sasha.

"Are you all set for our tour of Canada and the East Coast?" Alanah asked Sasha when they had some time together, sitting by the lake and watching campers take turns on the water-skiing tube being towed around by a speed boat. There wasn't a lot for Alanah to do, as there were experts taking charge of the activity. She and Sasha were on hand with the first aid kit.

Two campers had sped past their point on the shore, screaming with laughter, before Alanah realized Sasha hadn't answered. She turned to her friend. Had she heard the question?

"Don't ask again." Sasha held up her hand.

"Why? What's the matter?"

Sasha waved her hand up and down the length of her leg.

"But you've come to summer camp," Alanah said.

"I'm doped up on pain meds, I struggle to get from the cabin to anywhere, I'm going to have to do a load of physical therapy. I'm not going to be able to come, Alanah."

"But …"

"Six weeks of trying to climb aboard a bus, sitting at the bottom of the hiking trail while you go off with a handsome guide, not being able to do the therapy necessary to get this leg better ready for my wedding. I can't do it."

"But …"

"I want to do it. I do, Alanah, but I have to be practical. My coming with you would be a burden and would stop you from enjoying all the tourist things we'd planned to do."

"Not all of them."

"I need to stay and do the physical therapy when it's time."

"If you can't go, then I won't either. I don't want to go on my own."

"I've asked Lucy if she'd like to go in my place."

"Lucy?"

"I know she was just a kid when we lived in Australia, but she's fun, and she has the time, since her college is finished for the year. I'll transfer all of my reservations into her name."

Alanah paused. What could she say? She had been so excited about the six weeks of fun with her best friend.

"You'll still have fun seeing all the things you wanted to see, and Lucy is a great companion. I'm really sorry, Alanah. I wish it could have been different."

Alanah leaned close and gave Sasha a hug.

"I need you to video call every day, so you can see everything."

"I will. And don't worry. I will still get a fabulous holiday this year. Derek and I will have our honeymoon later in the year."

Alanah hugged her again. Derek and Sasha getting married. That was the whole reason she was here in the first place. "Just get better quickly. We don't want you still on crutches on your wedding day."

CHAPTER TEN

Alanah and Lucy were leaving for six weeks. Thank goodness. It was torture having her around, watching her laughing and flirting with Ryan Kozlanski. And now Caleb needed to make a determined effort to pour his attention on Kyla. It was summer and there were plenty of opportunities to spend Saturdays in the outdoors—together—just the two of them. Why didn't that thought thrill him? Stop. Just stop.

But the thoughts persisted, despite his best efforts.

"Hey, Caleb."

Caleb stepped out of the music shop and turned at the sound of his name being called. Jason Wainscott.

"Hey, Jason."

"Selena and I were wondering if you and Kyla wanted to get together for lunch after church on Sunday. Thought we'd grab some burgers and go out to the picnic ground for the afternoon."

Did he want to go on a picnic with another couple? He should jump at the chance.

"Is everything all right?" Jason must have sensed his hesitation.

"Do you have time right now?" Caleb asked. School was out, and Jason would have spare time away from his teacher's aide job. "I could use a listening ear."

"Sure."

"Meet you at Bellbird café in five?" Coffee and a mate. That seemed like what he needed right now.

Caleb soon sat opposite Jason at a small café table, with two strong coffees and choc chip cookies to meet his sugar cravings. He'd chosen a table near the back of the café, as he didn't want to be overheard.

"What's up, mate?"

"Kyla." Where should he begin?

"Are you guys okay? Is she okay?"

"I think I've made a mistake."

"What?" Jason's furrowed brow showed his concern.

Caleb couldn't seem to assemble the right words in a coherent order.

"Mate, you didn't …?"

"Didn't what?" That question sounded too accusatory, but then, it depended on what Jason was alluding to.

"You and Sasha's mate from Australia?"

"Alanah? What about her?"

"You haven't cheated on Kyla?"

"Wow. Thanks for your vote of confidence."

"Keep your hair on." Jason took a bite of his cookie. "It's just that Selena seemed to think you and Alanah have history, and that it might not be ancient history either."

Caleb took a decent slug of his coffee. Strong and bitter. Oh, for the Farmer's Union Iced Coffee. Shame Alanah didn't pack some of that in her luggage along with the Vegemite and Cherry Ripes. Great idea. Think about food … and Alanah.

"Caleb?"

Jason was still there, challenging him with a glare.

"I haven't cheated on Kyla."

"So what's your problem?"

"I shouldn't have asked Kyla to marry me."

"Because of Alanah?"

"I don't think I love Kyla—not like I should."

"This is just because your old girlfriend is here. You were okay before she arrived."

"No, I wasn't. The day I asked Kyla, I felt as if I was just going through the motions."

"Really?" That wasn't surprise in Jason's tone. It was another challenge.

"She'd been hinting and nagging me about it for so long, I thought I might just as well."

Jason rolled his eyes and shook his head.

"I know. I shouldn't have asked her. It was a mistake."

"Have you told her?"

"Not yet. She's been like an angry bear since Alanah got here—"

"With good reason."

"What good reason? Alanah and I have been mates since year seven."

"I forgot you went to high school in Australia. Brings back memories hearing you talk like that."

"Yeah, well, it brings back memories for me too. Alanah and I would have been a thing if my family hadn't moved back here."

"And you're considering her again."

"No."

"Truly?"

"Truly. On two counts. I'm engaged, and it could never work." Caleb took another sip of coffee.

"Why not?"

"Because Alanah would never shift away from her family. They're practically engraved in the Australian landscape." The inescapable obstacle confronted Caleb again.

"What about you?"

"I'm engaged."

"It sounds like you might not be for much longer."

"When my family came back to Trinity Lakes, it was for good. No, me and Alanah would never work."

"And Kyla? Don't you think you owe it to her to be truthful? Don't keep dragging it out if you're going to resent the relationship in the long run. You need to talk to her."

"I know."

"So what's keeping you?"

"I guess I wanted to wait until Alanah was long gone so that Kyla didn't blame her. It's not Alanah's fault."

"You're more concerned about Alanah than you are Kyla. That's a really bad look, mate."

"I know."

"My advice is you sort it out sooner rather than later."

"I know."

"So that's a 'no' to the Sunday picnic then?"

It was a "no" to Jason and Selena, but it was probably a good time to schedule a talk with Kyla. He had to be honest with her.

———

"DID THE EXPERIENCE MATCH YOUR EXPECTATIONS?" Lucy pushed her backpack beneath the ferry seat and settled down next to Alanah.

"Expectations?"

"Prince Edward Island. Was it what you thought it would be?"

"Yes and no." Alanah had watched the Megan Follows' version of *Anne of Green Gables* a few times. Her mother was a die-hard fan and had introduced Alanah to the habit early. Alanah had also watched the new series on Netflix and wasn't sure how to reconcile the two versions. They were both good but reaching a vastly different audience. Was it wrong to admit she preferred the 1980s version? The new Anne seemed determined to investigate all the social justice issues from the new millennium, and while that was interesting, it took away some of the child-like magic from the old.

"Where have you gone?" Lucy nudged her.

Alanah grinned. "Sorry. I was just reviewing my Anne-fan career."

"Mom is a fan," Lucy said.

"What about you?"

"I've watched it, of course …"

"Which version?"

"Both."

"Have you read the books?"

"Don't tell me you have?" Lucy turned her full grin in Alanah's direction.

"Only a couple, but I might read them all after today."

"Did you think the tourist activities did justice to the books and movie?"

"It was inspiring, but not the same as my imagination."

"That's a very Anne statement, if my memory serves."

"There were spots on the tour that I recognized from the '85 version of the film. It was a little off-putting to see the twenty-first century there as well. I think I prefer the fairyland that exists in my imagination."

"You're a lot like Sasha. That's the sort of thing she'd say."

"I hope she's all right," Alanah said. "I felt really bad coming on this trip without her. We'd been planning it for over a year."

"You feel bad? I feel worse. I'm having fun using the bookings she paid for."

"I'm glad you came. I couldn't have done this on my own."

Lucy gave a half laugh. "I'm glad I came, or you would have mown down half the freeway if I'd let you drive—on the wrong side of the road."

"That is only a matter of perspective, you know."

"Not to the cars heading towards you."

"Just wait until you're in Australia. Then we'll see how you go driving on the correct side of the road."

Lucy laughed and settled back into the seat.

"What are you going to do once you leave uni?" Alanah made herself comfortable as the ferry left the shores of Prince Edward Island.

"College." Lucy grinned.

"Yeah, I know. I just forget to use the US lingo."

"I'm not really sure, but I'd like to do something in the line of helping people."

"I did social work as a degree," Alanah said.

"And do you help people?"

"Not unless you count helping people pay their council rates and taking phone calls complaining about the state of the roads."

"No opportunities to do social work at Booleroo Whim?"

"There is, but it's not a huge demand. They usually get different workers come to the community center from Port Pirie. The job at the council is full time and pays the bills."

"You couldn't do social work part time?" Lucy held out a box of mints, and Alanah took one.

"There's so many government compliance issues," Alanah said, around her mint. "I'd have to set up on my own, and it would be more trouble than it's worth."

"So you do office administration?" What was that glimpse of doubt in Lucy's eyes?

"Okay. I admit it's not what I'd hoped for, but I hated living away from the farm, and travel to and from a larger town is prohibitive."

"You can't live on the farm your whole life, can you? What about Mitch?"

"At the moment, Mitch is on his own while Mum and Dad are touring Australia in a caravan."

"But he'll get married one day. Won't he take on the farm?"

Alanah was silent. It was the most likely scenario. Even in this day and age of equality, it was still expected that the son would become the farmer and take on the family business.

"Do you want to go into farming with your brother?"

Alanah shrugged. That was sort of what she did now. Whenever it was particularly busy—seeding, shearing, harvesting—she took as many days off as she had owing to pitch in. She loved it.

"You don't want to take on a farm of your own, do you?" Lucy asked.

Alanah shook her head. In all her daydreaming, she recognized how difficult it would be to do it on her own.

"I'm happy to be part of it, but Dad and Mitch are the full-time farmers."

"Why don't you marry a farmer? Have you got a boyfriend?"

A jolt.

"The men are a bit thin on the ground out our way. Most of the guys I went to school with are already in a relationship of some kind. Besides …"

"Besides?"

"There isn't anyone I am even remotely attracted to."

"I thought you and Caleb had a thing back in the day." There was something teasing in Lucy's tone.

Alanah swung a glance in her direction, small frown engaged and all.

Lucy shrugged. "Sorry. I just thought …"

"Well, we did have a thing back in the day, if you must know, but it fizzled out when your family moved back to the states."

Lucy grinned.

"What's that grin about?"

"It's not as fizzled as you think. I've seen the way Caleb acts when you're around."

"Caleb is engaged to Kyla."

"That won't last. I don't know why he asked her in the first place. I know they were friends and worked together in the youth group, but I never thought they would be a serious long-term relationship. I think he just got caught up in the idea of marriage."

"Really, Lucy. I don't think we should be speculating like this. Your brother is a caring guy. He's not going to trifle with Kyla's feelings."

"Trifle? There's a good old-fashioned word for you. Straight from Green Gables?"

"I prefer 'trifle' to other words that might only contain four letters, and start with ..."

"I get it. I prefer 'trifle' as well."

Alanah smiled and turned her head out to watch the passing seascape as they travelled towards Caribou, Nova Scotia.

———

THE EAST COAST attractions were done and dusted. They'd visited the American cities before going to P.E.I., and Alanah had decided New York was overrated. She hadn't been sorry to leave the overcrowded metropolis full of crazy street buskers. Boston had been quaint and interesting, and of course, P.E.I. had been the highlight. P.E.I. had been the whole reason to come east in the first place. But now it was time to head back west. She couldn't wait to get to the great outdoors. Banff was calling, and her expectations were high. She hoped the brochures did the trip justice.

Spending this time with Lucy had helped form yet another bond with the Kennedy family. Lucy had only been twelve when they were last in Australia, and Alanah hadn't connected with her then. The distance between a seventeen-year-old and a twelve-year-old was immense. Now Lucy was twenty-four, they were both young adults, and Alanah found she was enjoying her company as much as she would have Sasha—or Caleb.

Actually, spending time with Caleb was torture. Who was she kidding? She was still crazy about the guy, but even if it hadn't been for Kyla, their homelands were too far apart. That fact remained as immovable as the Canadian Rockies.

Focus on today. The scenery in the Rockies was magnificent. Breathtaking. Awesome. Words were not doing the experience justice. Best to soak up the majesty of the glassy lakes and snow-covered peaks while she could—and stop thinking about a relationship that was doomed a decade ago.

———

THIS WAS SUCH A BAD IDEA. Jason had asked Caleb to join him and his fiancée on a picnic, which he'd declined. Without thinking it through, Caleb had decided to take Kyla on a picnic to have that honest talk. What an idiot. Picnics were classified as a romantic activity. Kyla was ecstatic. Her face shone with smiles. She was in a light-hearted mood—chatting merrily, playing upbeat music. He wasn't going to be able to introduce the honest talk to her now.

"I'm glad to have you back." Kyla kissed him on the cheek as he stood up from retrieving the picnic basket from the trunk.

Her statement rankled, but her whole demeanor today was so light and happy he didn't have the heart to call her on it.

Grabbing his free hand, Kyla pulled him forward across the parking lot. "There's a brilliant spot down by the lake I know of."

Caleb followed without comment. Today Kyla was at her most attractive. She was dressed in jeans with a close-fitting white t-shirt that showed off her trim and athletic figure. Her white sneakers added to the fresh effect, and a mustard-colored sweater was draped over her shoulders, with the arms tied loosely at the front. Could he marry her? Her dark hair, tied back in a bouncy ponytail, was beautiful, and her dark eyes sparkled against the colors of her outfit. She was attractive. Was he mad for thinking of ending their relationship?

One thing was for sure, taking her on a picnic was not the right way to break up with her—if he was going to do it. He took a deep breath.

"Isn't this fresh air invigorating?" Kyla had noticed.

Thank goodness she'd taken his deep breath of contemplation as a sign of his absorbing the beauty of the day. He nodded and smiled. He couldn't break up with her today. It wasn't the right time. And maybe, now that Alanah was in Canada, he could free himself of thoughts about his childhood sweetheart. Alanah would be headed back to the other side of the world in a month or so. It was best he leave well enough alone. Kyla was here and she was lovely—today.

CHAPTER ELEVEN

"So glad I'm used to riding horseback." Alanah turned to Lucy who rode alongside her. They were in a convoy of horses following the trail guide along one of the mountain paths in Jasper National Park.

"I haven't ridden horseback since I was in Australia." Lucy twisted and adjusted in her saddle. The four-hour ride was obviously taking its toll. Alanah was feeling a bit stiff herself. She rode droving sheep on occasion. Not so much for pleasure. She hadn't been four hours in the saddle for some time. She'd probably be stiff in the morning.

"Sasha would have loved this," Lucy said.

"She would have."

"I still feel guilty taking her trip."

"She wouldn't have been able to do any of this, Lucy. Not the hiking or the canoeing or the horse riding. We would have had to sit out of all of it, because I wouldn't have left her alone in the accommodation for all these outings."

Alanah closed her eyes for a few moments, confident her horse would continue following the pack. This was her last day in the Canadian Rockies region. Tonight they would take the bus back to Calgary, and tomorrow they would fly back to Walla Walla. The last six weeks of touring with Lucy had been magical, even without Sasha. They were due to arrive back on the third of July, and there would be loads of family activity going on. Fireworks on the fourth. Sasha's wedding to get prepared for. And Caleb. The thought of him was both a downer and excited darts of anticipation—all at the same time. Talk about cognitive dissonance.

Alanah jolted forward and opened her eyes with a start. Why had her horse stopped? Everyone's horse had stopped, yet no one was talking. Alanah turned toward Lucy who had her finger to her lips, then she pointed across to the edge of the clearing. A bear. A grizzly? The guide at the front had halted the group and appeared to be waiting to see if the bear would retreat from them. They certainly weren't going to push forward to threaten the animal.

What was she supposed to have remembered about possible encounters with bears? Stay still. Don't panic. Where was that can of bear spray? She felt for it on her walking belt. But the guide seemed to know his business. He didn't seem to be particularly alarmed about the dangerous animal not more than thirty meters away.

"A grizzly." Lucy mouthed the words with no sound. Alanah nodded. The guide had said it was incredibly rare to see a grizzly in the wild, and they should count themselves fortunate if they did. She'd agree, so long as the bear didn't charge and eat one of them.

Suddenly the bear seemed to sense them as a threat—or at least it focused directly at them and rose on its hind legs.

"Uh oh!" Alanah couldn't keep the comment to herself. Others in the tour group used stronger four-lettered words that held the same amount of angst.

"Don't panic," Lucy said in a low tone.

Sure. Good advice. Then the bear dropped on all fours and

charged. Before the shrieks could break out, the tour guide yelled in a firm tone, "Be calm!"

As his low and firm voice rang out, the bear stopped, swinging its head and growling, before turning tail and moving back into the trees. Was that it? Alanah's heart was still hammering at an alarming rate.

"She was just testing her dominance." The guide didn't appear to be shaken and had turned his horse on the trail to face the mounted tourists. "You folks were given a treat today."

"Speak for yourself," Lucy said under her breath.

"It's not often I see a beautiful creature like that on the rides."

Alanah sucked in another lungful of air. Now the bear had disappeared and the group of riders had settled, her heart rate resumed normal pace.

"Have you seen many bears before?" Alanah asked Lucy.

"Can't say that I have, to be honest." Lucy k-kitched her horse into motion again. "I saw more dangerous creatures in Australia than I've seen here."

"What? We don't have bears."

"Snakes, crocodiles, sharks."

"You did not see sharks."

Lucy laughed.

"Or crocodiles. You're making that up."

"We saw crocodiles when we visited the Australia Zoo in Queensland."

"Seeing a croc in captivity is a different thing to seeing a creature unrestrained in the wild."

"What about the snakes? You can't deny there are snakes everywhere near your place."

"A few, but they're easier to avoid than a charging grizzly."

"And drop bears." Lucy laughed.

Alanah laughed with her. Gullible foreign tourists worried the infamous drop bear would fall on their head, ready to rip their throats out. An Aussie hoax which—for some strange reason—had a lot of traction. Even if they had been real, they weren't as terrifying as a real-life grizzly bear.

The ride back down the trail to the tour bus was uneventful. Alanah inhaled a deep breath, still surrounded by the magnificent Canadian forest. The smell of pine and spruce was so different to the wattle and eucalyptus of the Australian bush. Both beautiful but in vastly different ways.

Once they'd dismounted on jelly-legs, said goodbye to their mounts, and returned to the tour bus, Alanah was ready for her evening meal and bed.

"I've had such a good time, Lucy. Thank you for coming. This has been the trip of a lifetime."

"Thanks for letting me come. I might live here now, but you know how it is. The locals never travel in their own region. I've really enjoyed it too."

As they approached the bus, something seemed off.

"There's police at the bus." Lucy increased her pace as she spoke.

What could they be there for? Alanah did a quick scout around their group, counting members. Had they left someone behind somewhere? She checked back towards the bus and the cops talking to the tour guide.

"Someone's broken into the bus." Another tourist turned back and spread the news.

"Are you sure? How do you know?" Alanah asked.

The tourist pointed toward the bus. On closer inspection, Alanah could see that one of the lower windows near the front was smashed. What could they have wanted? If they'd wanted to steal the bus, they'd failed, because it was still here.

Then it hit her. She'd left her larger backpack under her seat, only taking the smaller pack for the water bottle and lunch. Surely they wouldn't have taken a backpack. Would they?

"What's the matter?" Lucy asked. "You've gone all pale."

"I left my larger backpack on the bus under my seat."

Lucy's visage became serious.

"I had my wallet and passport in there," Alanah said.

"What! Why?"

"Didn't you leave yours in your luggage?"

"No, I put it in my fanny pack." Lucy patted the small of her back. Obviously the bum-bag was hidden beneath her t-shirt.

"I thought the bus was secure." A sense of dread crept higher in Alanah's throat.

"Let's not borrow trouble. They might have been after something else." Lucy put a comforting hand on Alanah's shoulder, which did almost nothing to alleviate her worry.

"I hope so."

"Come on," Lucy said, taking Alanah by the arm and pulling her forward. "Let's find out the worst."

As they stepped close enough to hear the conversation, the bus driver turned to the assembled group of tourists. Where had he been while the bus was being broken into?

"Folks, I'm sorry to report there has been a break-in on our bus." Thank you, captain, obvious. "It appears to have been a group of kids rifling through personal belongings to see if they could find anything valuable. I would imagine they got away with very little." It was all right for him to say. Depends on what he considered valuable. "If you are worried about anything, please step forward and we will discuss it with the police constable."

Lucy tugged Alanah forward to the front of the group. They were two of about six people with worried expressions.

"She left her backpack with wallet and passport under her seat." Lucy offered the information first.

"Can you tell us your seat number, please?" It would have been a great tourist coup, talking to a member of the Royal Canadian Mounted Police, if it weren't for her anxiety.

"Seat seven A. She wanted the window seat."

Thank you, Lucy. This handsome cop was going to think she was non-verbal at this rate.

"And can you describe the backpack?"

"Plain black, but I had a red-polka-dot ribbon attached to the zipper." At last she'd found her voice, and now was the time to scrape her dignity back together. How could she have left her credit card, cash, and passport behind? Because she thought they were out in the bush—forest—where there was nothing but squirrels, chipmunks, and the occasional grizzly bear. There was a small kiosk diner in the carpark. Obviously the bus driver had gone to eat and watch the sports news on the telly above the bar. *Stupid, stupid, stupid.*

"Is this it?" The constable stepped down from the bus holding her backpack. The relief nearly knocked her over.

"Check to make sure everything is inside." Lucy. The voice of reason.

Alanah took her pack and, with shaking fingers, she unzipped the compartment where she kept everything important. The relief leaked away like water from a bathtub. Her travel wallet with cash, credit card, and passport, was gone.

"Are you all right?" Handsome Mounties were all very well, but this was not the time for flirting.

"Alanah? Do you need to sit down?" Lucy guided her to the step of the bus.

"Is something missing from your bag?" The Mountie squatted down at her level.

"My travel wallet."

"Cash, cards?" His gaze held compassion.

"And passport."

Lucy inhaled a deep breath. "They won't let you back into the US without a passport."

Alanah noticed the small frown the constable cast to Lucy. He was trying to make this less stressful.

"Hey. I need to check to see if my stuff is okay as well." A man behind Lucy shouldered past her. "This Aussie isn't the only one who might have had stuff nicked." His accent gave him away as being from the UK.

"Yes, sir. If you could be patient, I will check all the things, but I need to make sure we don't disturb evidence."

Somehow Lucy managed to get Alanah to move to the picnic table in the clearing near the car park. Everything had turned to a muted misty grey in Alanah's mind. What was she going to do?

Click. Click. Lucy snapped her fingers in front of Alanah's eyes. It took some doing, but she readjusted her brain and focused in on Lucy's face.

"We have to make a plan," Lucy said.

"Maybe they'll catch the culprit and return my stuff."

"It doesn't seem like they've got the bloodhounds out trying to track anyone down. We need to call Mom and Dad. They'll tell us what to do."

Alanah nodded. She couldn't think straight. Mr. and Mrs. Kennedy would help her figure this mess out.

———

A KNOCK on his bedroom door roused Caleb. He'd crashed on his bed the minute he'd walked through the door from work. It had been a full-on week. With the Fourth of July parade set for two days' time, there were music students wanting extra rehearsal time, parents wanting instruments serviced—new strings, new reeds—any manner of musical things needed sharpening up ready for the parade. He was glad he wasn't actually playing anything this year. He might have been an instrumental tutor, but the high school band would take center stage and they would be led by their school music teacher. The knock sounded on the door again.

"Yes. I'm coming." He threw his legs over the side of the bed as his mother opened the door. "Is dinner ready?"

"Not yet." Mom looked worried.

"What's the matter?"

"The girls have been robbed."

"Which girls?" Alanah was his first thought, but he had two sisters still at home. Sasha wasn't likely to be out and about, but Mia …?

"Lucy and Alanah."

Caleb shot up from the bed, alert and dreading what else he may hear.

"Are they all right? Were they attacked?"

"Calm down." Mom's controlled approach was infuriating sometimes. "Someone broke into the tour bus while they were on a horseback ride through the national park."

"But they're all right?"

Mom nodded. "Alanah's travel wallet and passport have been stolen. She won't be able to get out of Canada until she's got a replacement passport."

"How long will that take? They were due to fly back tomorrow."

"Lucy will fly home. She has to get back to work. Dad and I are trying to figure out which one of us will drive up there to get Alanah, and take her to Vancouver."

"Vancouver?"

"That's the nearest Australian embassy, apparently. Hopefully they'll rush a replacement passport through."

"You won't be able to get there and back before the parade."

Mom nodded again. "I realize that."

"Aren't you and Dad involved with the parade?"

She nodded again.

"You want me to go." It was more a statement than a question.

"Sasha can't drive, and Matt and Mia aren't as close to Alanah as you."

"I'm not sure it's a good idea." He'd tentatively decided to push through with Kyla. Going off on a rescue trip after Alanah would cause pain on so many levels.

"If you can't, then we'll have to think of something else, but Alanah only has tonight's accommodation paid for. It will take time for her bank to issue her another credit card, which she will probably have to have FedExed here. She's kind of stuck."

"We could transfer money to Lucy's card so she can leave Alanah with the cash she needs."

Mom twisted her mouth into a thoughtful shape, then shook her head. "We could, Caleb, but it's more about leaving Alanah alone in a foreign country to deal with a problem. If it were me, I'd be stressed and overwhelmed."

She was right, of course. Sending money was easy, but it didn't make up for emotional and moral support.

"No, I think one of us will have to set out to be there at least by the time of tomorrow morning's checkout. What do you think?" Was Mom really asking his opinion or was this more an announcement of strategy?

"Where are they now?"

"They'll spend tonight in Calgary. Then Alanah will go to the airport on the shuttle with Lucy, also pre-paid. Someone needs to meet her there."

"Wouldn't it be quicker for one of us to fly to Calgary and hire a car to take from there to Vancouver. Better still, couldn't Alanah fly to Vancouver and one of us meet her there?"

"It would be quicker for sure, but cost is still a factor. Flights and car hire don't come cheap, and Alanah would have to pay for her replacement flights, which will be more expensive since she'd be booking at the last minute and its vacation time. Until her new card is released, we will have to spring for the whole rescue mission—her flights and ours. Our budget isn't looking that great to be adding all those extra expenses at the moment. Alanah won't have access to her funds for a number of days, even if she does have emergency cash."

"What about her travel insurance?"

"I suppose she has it, but that isn't likely to pay out any sooner. Those sorts of things take forever to process."

"You want me to go, don't you?"

"Honestly, Caleb, it would be the best solution to the problem. We can't leave Alanah stranded in a foreign country with no money. The car trip will take a lot longer, but we can afford the gas."

"Kyla is expecting me to spend the holiday with her."

"Take her with you."

Right. Sure. What a great idea. Kyla would burst into flames the minute she realized they were driving to rescue Alanah.

"If you're going to marry that girl, you're going to have to know that the two of you are secure in your relationship."

"Which girl?" Whoops. He'd let that slip.

"Kyla. What other girl is there?"

Caleb shrugged.

"I'll talk to Kyla and see what she says, but I'm not promising anything."

"Can you talk to her now? We need to reassure Alanah that help is on the way."

Mom closed the bedroom door. Caleb sat back down, exhaling a lungful of frustration. He didn't want to call Kyla. He knew her well enough to know that asking for her help was going to result in a full-on emotional confrontation. He didn't have the energy for that.

Perhaps he should just go on his own and tell her he had an emergency he needed to deal with. Well, it was an emergency. He could throw a fit and tell his parents to pull out of their Fourth of July responsibilities. Or he could just make the decision and do what was best.

"Mom." He walked up behind her as she was pulling the fried chicken from the pan onto a kitchen towel.

"What did she say?" Mom continued to rescue the golden-brown coated chicken from the oil.

"I'll go on my own."

"Kyla doesn't want to come?"

"I'm not going to ask her. She's got family plans over the holiday. It's easier if I just make the decision and help Alanah out."

CHAPTER TWELVE

The drive from Trinity Lakes to Calgary would take around ten hours. Considering the whole drama was about a lost passport, he remembered to pack his passport along with a small overnight bag. His mother provided a stock of snacks and food for the trip, and he brewed some strong coffee to help keep him awake. Lucy's flight was due to leave at midday from Calgary, so he'd set his alarm for two in the morning, so he would arrive just as Lucy left.

Getting to sleep last night had been difficult. Going to bed at eight thirty, when it was still light, was part of it, but worrying about what Kyla would say when she found out was what kept him awake. In the end, he managed four hours sleep before he'd set out. Not nearly enough. He hoped Alanah had slept well, because he was going to get her to drive once they connected. Maybe he should have brought Kyla along as a second driver, but would it have been worth the drama? Too late now. It was close to seven in the morning, and he was approaching the Canadian border.

There was a bit of a queue at the border, but no issue for him showing his US passport and crossing over. According to his GPS, it was at least another five hours to Calgary Airport. He was cutting it fine if he wanted to be there by the time Lucy flew out, but he needed to have a pit stop and stretch his legs for a few minutes. Some fresh coffee wouldn't hurt either.

He was back on BC-95 by eight. He had his music playing on a playlist that was energetic and likely to cause him to tap out the rhythm on the steering wheel. The freeway was designed for easy traffic flow, but the majestic scenery was a little too far away to become immersed in it. He kept an eye on his dashboard clock. He needed to get to Calgary before midday, but that seemed less likely as the time passed. At least he was wide awake. That last double-shot espresso probably had something to do with it.

At 9:13 a.m. the phone rang. Kyla. Should he answer it? Of course, he should, but did he want to face Kyla's questions? He rejected the call. But thirty seconds later, she called again. She wouldn't quit easily.

"Hi." He tried to inject enthusiasm into his tone.

"What on earth are you doing in Canada?"

"How did you know I was in Canada?"

"That friend location sharing app."

Caleb racked his brains. When had he shared his location finder with Kyla?

"I didn't know you had me on a locator app."

"When we arranged that car rally a couple of years ago, we all shared in case we got lost."

Right. Of course. He had never used it, but apparently Kyla was not above stalking his whereabouts. He felt bad even as the thought crossed his mind. She was his fiancée. If anyone had a right to know where he was, she did.

"Why are you in Canada?"

"I'm on a mission for Mom and Dad."

"Mission? It's the Fourth of July tomorrow. What could they need you to do in Canada?"

"They sent me to help someone out of a situation."

"Not Alanah, I hope. I thought we were well rid of her."

"Kyla! Alanah is not a person who I will ever be rid of. She's a family friend, and at the moment she's in trouble."

"For goodness sake, Caleb. What sort of sob story has she sent you this time?"

"I don't like your attitude."

"I don't like you running after her every time she crooks her little finger."

"She was robbed, if you must know."

"Is she injured? In hospital?"

"No. She is stranded. No passport to get home, and no money to get to Vancouver for a new passport."

"Honestly, Caleb. Why didn't Lucy help her sort it out? She was already there."

"Lucy has already taken several weeks off work and had promised to be back."

"You promised you'd spend the next couple of days with me and my family."

"The way you're going on, I don't have any wish to spend any time with you, or your family, Kyla. You need to stop being so possessive. It's not nice."

"We are going to be married, Caleb. Don't you get it? I'm going to be your wife. Until death us do part. Intimate loving partners for life."

Something soured in Caleb's throat. The very idea of marriage to her was distasteful. This was his fault. He should have told her at their picnic.

"Caleb?"

What was he supposed to say? At moments like this it was clear. Her reaction to Alanah, making him feel guilty about anything he did with her, was a massive problem in their relationship.

"It's me or her, Caleb. I'm not going to share you."

"What?" Had she just delivered an ultimatum?

"You heard me. You need to make a decision. Either you turn around and come back and fulfill your promise to me, or you can consider this relationship over."

"Really? You're going to emotionally blackmail me?"

"What's it going to be?" Her tone was cold, ruthless.

"That's easy. I'd choose Alanah's friendship any day over this sort of rubbish. If that's how you want it, Kyla, then so be it. We're finished."

———

"Here, let me share Caleb's number with you." Alanah's phone pinged as a message came in from Lucy. "Mom said he would try to be here by midday."

It was eleven thirty, and Lucy's flight was boarding. Another half hour before Caleb was likely to arrive. It was a little disconcerting being left in a foreign country with no passport, and only the small amount of cash Lucy had given her.

"I've had the best time with you, Alanah. Sasha is going to be so jealous." Lucy hugged her firmly. "Don't worry. Caleb will help you get this all sorted out, and we'll see you in a few days."

"I'm going to miss Independence Day."

"There may be some Americans here who will celebrate. Caleb will celebrate with you."

That thought was attractive and alarming all at the same time.

"Final boarding call for Alaska Air flight to Walla Walla. Could all passengers please report to Gate 45 for immediate boarding."

Worry gripped Alanah's stomach as Lucy gathered her hand luggage and reached out for one last hug.

"Go down to the arrivals area and give Caleb a call. I'm sure he won't be too far away."

Alanah smiled weakly at Lucy as she joined the line through security and on to the gate to board her flight. The flight Alanah should also have been boarding.

Once Lucy was no longer visible, Alanah turned to head back through the terminal to the arrivals area, dragging her suitcase behind her. Should she grab something for lunch or wait for Caleb, so they could eat together? She decided she would call him and see how far away he was.

The phone rang multiple times, but he didn't answer. No need to panic—just yet. She went to a small airport café and ordered a hot chocolate. She'd had too much coffee already, and the sugar would stave off her lunchtime hunger pangs.

After she'd settled on one of the airport bench seats, she tried Caleb's number again. It was just after midday. He must be close.

"Hello, this is Caleb." That tone was a bit short, but he probably didn't know it was her because he wouldn't have her number saved in his phone. Why would he?

"Hi, Caleb. This is Alanah. Just wondering how far away you are. I can see the area outside for car rentals. I can meet you there."

"I thought Mom said I'd meet you around twelve?"

"It's five past twelve now." Why did he sound so irritable?

"It's five past eleven. I'm still at least an hour and a half away."

Alanah checked her watch, anxiety beginning to nest in her stomach. "Alberta is an hour in front of British Columbia. Did you change your watch?" She'd done this when they arrived from Banff yesterday.

Was that silence, or did she hear him curse under his breath.

"It's okay, Caleb. I'll buy myself lunch. Lucy left me some cash. Call me when you're five minutes away and I'll meet you at the car rental area."

"Sorry, Alanah. I didn't factor in the time zone change, and I've had a bad morning."

"No worries. I'll see you soon." She disconnected the call. Had a bad morning? What could be so bad, other than having to get out of bed in the middle of the night and drive eleven hours across country. That was a reason for short temper, maybe. Her heart softened again. It was like as if she had to drive from Booleroo Whim to Melbourne on a moment's notice. Not a short drive by anyone's standards. She decided to cut him some slack. He was giving up his Independence Day with Kyla.

———

HE WAS SUCH AN IDIOT. He knew Alberta was an hour in front of Washington and BC, but he hadn't thought about it when his mother had asked him to drive. Not that it mattered much. They weren't going to be able to make the Australian consulate in Vancouver before close of business today ... which produced a new problem. They were going to have to stay overnight somewhere, an expense neither of them could afford.

He had a swag in the back of his truck which might sort the problem for him, but it wasn't appropriate for them both. The swag made him think of Australia again. Australians had used swags for camping for years, but it was only in recent times he'd seen them available in the camping stores here. He'd bought one straight away, even if for old times' sake. It sat in the back of his truck, rarely used, but he would use it tonight. He had to figure out a suitable arrangement for Alanah.

Caleb slammed his palm on the steering wheel again. He'd just effectively ended his relationship with Kyla while driving at maximum speed to pick up Alanah. His feelings were all over the place. It was a relief to have broken up with Kyla, but he felt guilty at the same time. Added to his guilt was the thought of seeing Alanah pricking at the back of his mind, sending jolts of anticipation leaking into his consciousness. But he had to shut that down, because thinking of Alanah in any way at all should bring no emotion. Nothing.

That should be the case but wasn't. Guilt leapt out and pounced on him again. He should be devastated over his broken engagement, and he should feel nothing but annoyance at having to rescue Alanah. Nothing was as it should be—except the guilt.

The miles passed quickly at the speed limit, bringing him closer to Alanah. He needed to get himself sorted. He had been a bit short on the phone before. She was a good friend, and he was going to be spending the next couple of days in close contact with her. It was time to be pleasant. He could do pleasant.

The GPS said he was ten minutes away from the Calgary Airport, so he pressed the number on the recent calls screen.

"You nearly here?" Alanah's voice was cheery at least.

"Ten minutes away. I'll find the car rental parking lot."

"Right. I'll head in that direction now ... and Caleb, thanks for doing this. I know it must be a huge pain."

"My pleasure."

My pleasure? He disconnected the call. It was true. He would drive these three long trips and enjoy every moment of it, whether it was right to do so or not. He loved Alanah. Always had. Future or no future, she was the person he most wanted to be with.

He took the exit off the freeway leading to the airport and wrestled with the ethical argument raging in his head. Be distant. Don't let yourself be involved. She's going back to Australia. You're only making this harder for yourself.

Ha! Like he didn't know all that. But he wasn't going to

endure the next couple of days refusing to engage with her. They would just have to talk about it. Lay the cards on the table and move forward as best they could.

She wasn't hard to spot. Did she stand out or was he particularly sensitive to her? She wasn't wearing anything different to other people milling about. Her suitcase was a normal bland color, so he had to assume he was hyper-aware when it came to her. He pulled into the parking bay closest to her, killed the engine and got out. Was it appropriate to hug her? Not even, but he did anyway.

"Are you all right?" He lifted her suitcase and hefted it over the side of his truck.

"Much better now you're here."

What did she mean by that? He was not going to ask.

"I panicked when I realized my passport had been stolen. Lucy was great, but when she left, I felt all alone in a foreign land."

That's what she meant. Not that she was desperate to see him. Anybody from the Kennedy household would probably suffice.

"You must be wrecked," Alanah said as she opened the driver's side door.

What was she doing? He was wrecked, but …

"Do you have a license to drive in America?"

"What? Oh …" She grinned and looked up after peering inside the cabin. "I'm used to this being the passenger side. "But since I'm here. Do you want me to drive?"

Did he? The last time they'd driven together was in Australia, on back roads. She'd just got her license, and though they often drove in the middle of the country roads to avoid potholes, according to Australian road law she should always drive on the left-hand side of the road. It had taken him a while to adjust to driving on the right-hand side.

"You don't seem confident," she said, grinning again.

"Do you have an international license?"

"I did apply for something of the sort from the RAA before I left Australia."

"Have you driven here yet?"

She shook her head. "How hard can it be?"

"You mean other than driving on the other side of the road, and all the turns that are counterintuitive to what you've learned?"

Alanah walked around to the passenger side. "I get it. I'm happy to be a passenger."

Caleb got in the driver's seat, set his GPS to the Australian Embassy in Vancouver, and pressed start.

"That's ten and a half hours drive." She sounded surprised as she examined the dashboard screen.

"I think we'll stop to eat first."

"Caleb, you need to rest a while. It's dangerous, driving when you're so fatigued."

"Let's find a truck stop somewhere, get some food, and I'll take a short nap while you eat."

"When are you going to eat?"

She was processing this step by step. He shrugged and pulled away from the curb.

Eat first, take forty-winks and then plot out the rest of the plan.

―――

ROADSIDE FAST FOOD TASTED GREAT. Hunger did that to food—made it more appealing than it probably was. Alanah hadn't said anything when Caleb had driven nearly three hours before he decided to stop for lunch. It was closer to dinnertime. He was obviously famished, putting away a burger, fries, and several other unidentifiable pieces of fried food. He'd lain down on the grass next to the truck and shut his eyes. Alanah didn't have the heart to wake him, but it was after five o'clock and she wasn't confident they should continue driving into the night with him having started so early in the morning.

She pulled out her phone and searched for nearby campgrounds. There was a trailer park about ten miles from where they were. She was happy to sleep in the cabin of the truck and let Caleb roll out his swag.

She went back into the truck stop area and bought some fruit and sandwiches. Lucy's money was now officially gone. She had to wait until she got her new card from the bank before she could start using her own money again.

"There you are." Caleb was standing next to the truck when she came back. "I woke up and you were gone, and I had a moment of panic."

"All good. I was just getting some food to tide us over."

"I suppose we'd better get back on the road."

"You were dead to the world a moment ago. I think we should probably find a camping spot and sleep for the night. The embassy won't be open until nine tomorrow morning, so we could set out again around five and get there in the late morning."

"I'm not sure about camping ..."

"There's a campground not far from here. I'll sleep in the cab of the truck, and you can sleep in the swag in the back of the truck."

"You've got it all sorted out."

What was that in his tone?

"Sorry. I didn't mean to take charge. I'm happy to do what you think is best."

"Really?"

There was a distinct sarcasm in his tone.

"Caleb Kennedy, I'm just trying to be proactive, and I don't want to put so much stress on you. But if you feel confident to drive overnight, then I'll try and stay awake to keep you company." She didn't try to hide her reaction. He'd been fractious ever since he'd picked her up.

"I'm sorry."

"I know you've made a huge sacrifice to come to my rescue, and I feel bad. I really do. But we're here now, so could we try to make the best of it?"

"You're right. We should find somewhere to camp. I'm exhausted."

"Great." She tried to inject enthusiasm into her tone, though she was still annoyed at his mood.

"Alanah?"

"Yes?"

"I broke up with Kyla this morning."

The words took a moment to register, then all sorts of emotions ran riot, crashing into different thoughts that launched like horses from a starting gate. That was terrible news. That was amazing news. She was so sorry. She was so happy. This was ridiculous. Poor Caleb.

"I'm really sorry, Caleb. You must feel awful."

He didn't say anything but followed the road the GPS recommended.

"I'm sorry you've had to come all this way. Do you think it can be worked out when you get back and have a chance to talk to her face to face?" Alanah cast a glance in his direction, trying to gauge what was going on in his mind.

His jaw tightened.

"What?"

"Nothing."

"What, Caleb? I know it's something."

"She gave me an ultimatum."

"About what?"

More strained silence. Alanah twisted on her bench seat and fixed her focus on him.

"I was halfway here, and she said I either had to turn around or it was over."

"But ..."

"She said it was either you or her." His teeth were clenched.

"Did it really have to come to that? You told her there was nothing between us, right?"

"Isn't there?"

"What?"

"Anything between us?"

"We have history. A friendship."

"Is that all?"

"Yes. That has to be all, Caleb. We've talked about this. Nothing has changed for either of us. There is no future for us."

He pulled the truck off to the side of the road, applied the handbrake and turned to face her, but didn't say anything.

"You had a future with Kyla." Alanah hated saying the words, but it was true.

He continued to stare at her, rolling his lips until they disappeared. "I could not have gone on with Kyla. I've been regretting that relationship pretty much from the moment we got engaged."

"Then this isn't about me, is it? I didn't break you up?"

He didn't say anything.

"Caleb, please. Don't let me be the one who has ruined your best chance at happiness."

"You're kidding yourself, Alanah. I left my best chance at happiness nearly twelve years ago when I returned to Trinity Lakes."

"Caleb, don't."

She should turn away, but his gorgeous blue eyes were pleading. She couldn't break her gaze, even if she tried. If there wasn't the distance of another passenger seat between them, she would be drawn into his vortex of wanting—needing—to be together. But the distance was there, and something sensible prevented her from crossing over into his reach.

A car speeding past so fast it rocked the truck broke the spell.

"We need to keep going, Caleb."

"I think we should drive overnight."

Alanah nodded. There was nothing to be gained by them sitting in friendly conversation over a sandwich and settling down for the night—nothing except blessed sleep.

CHAPTER THIRTEEN

Alanah breathed a sigh of relief as they approached the outskirts of Vancouver at about two thirty. They'd stopped for coffee and a toilet break a couple of times. Caleb had cranked the music for some of the drive. Alanah had wanted to sing, but there was a strange tension between them now. Even talking about ordinary things seemed difficult. What was the point in talking about hopes and dreams and things about life when what they probably both wanted was to share life—and they couldn't.

Alanah had punctuated the darkness every now and then with the question: "Are you okay?"

"So far so good."

The answer was devoid of emotion. It was probably a stupid idea to drive fatigued, but there it was.

And now they were at their destination in the dark of night, with nowhere to sleep.

"Should I see if I can find another caravan park?"

"Wouldn't it be too late to check in?"

"Probably. What about a car park somewhere?"

"Parking lot."

Was he correcting her language?

"Caleb. I'm sorry. I can't change the way things are. Can you?"

Suddenly Caleb took an exit from the freeway. Alanah noted the signs for a services stop. They could park there and grab some sleep.

As they pulled into the car park—parking lot if you were going to be antsy and pedantic—Alanah searched for the loo. Several hours of driving and too many coffees were doing their work. But before she could get out of the truck, Caleb reached across and touched her arm.

"Caleb ..."

"No, listen, Alanah. You're right. I know it. And besides, what sort of lowlife am I even thinking of someone other than Kyla? I only broke up with her this morning. I know I'm out of sorts. I'm sorry."

"Well, yeah ..."

"Let's just get you to the embassy first thing in the morning, get you sorted, and then we can get you home."

"Get me back to Trinity Lakes." She hated to contradict him, but Booleroo Whim, South Australia, was her home.

"Back to my home." Caleb turned and got out of the truck. She'd made her point, and he didn't like it. But it was as it was.

Alanah searched the opening times of the Australian Embassy. It was the Fourth of July, American Independence Day. But that was an American holiday. This was Canada. She'd already managed to offend a number of Canadians by assuming what happened in the US also happened in Canada. Canada also had a National Day holiday, but it wasn't on the same day the Americans celebrated, so she'd been told.

Her search revealed that the Australian Embassy opened at nine. Another six hours to wait, hopefully to get some sleep. Her search also revealed it could take as long as two working days to get an emergency replacement passport. Worry threatened to squeeze a band around her forehead, but she cast it off. There was nothing to be gained by worrying. She would just do what she had to do and be thankful she was not on her own.

"I'm going to lie down in the back of the truck." Caleb was unrolling his swag. She was not going to begrudge him that since he'd been driving for nearly twenty-four hours.

"No worries. I'll lie down in the cabin for a while."

She climbed in and fussed with her backpack, trying to form some sort of pillow. But it didn't matter too much. She was craving sleep.

———

SUNLIGHT DRILLED into Caleb's eyelids, waking him. He groaned, glancing at his watch. Just after five. That was the trouble with the height of summer. Early sunrise. It would have been okay if he'd been home in his bed, with the blackout shades drawn. He was not ready to be awake by a long shot, and still had four hours before they needed to get to the embassy. He pulled the canvas cover over his head and tried to drift back to sleep.

Two seconds later, he was jolted back to wakefulness by the sound of the truck cabin door opening and closing. Alanah. She'd obviously tried not to slam the door, but it was enough to disturb him. He glanced at his watch again. Amazing how two seconds had actually been two hours. He didn't feel any less hung over from sleep deprivation. Should he let her know he was awake? Just another hour of sleep.

He relaxed back into his swag again and allowed sleep to cloud his brain. With so many troubling thoughts in his consciousness, he wanted to avoid being awake and having to deal with them. They intruded anyway. He'd messed up with Kyla big time. He should never have asked her to marry him. He'd known it almost the second the words had come out of his mouth but had told himself she was a nice girl. She was a Christian and enthusiastic about serving God. Could he have made it work?

It's either me or her.

That was the kicker. Her insecurity about Alanah. Her controlling possessiveness.

Would Kyla have been better once Alanah went back home?

Maybe. But how long would it be before she found something else to be jealous about. Was this part of her character?

He was an idiot. Why had he asked her?

And now he was here with Alanah. How he wanted to hold her, kiss her, be with her forever. It was torture. Maybe she'd consider leaving Australia permanently now that they were older.

Stop being selfish. Alanah was close to her parents, her sister, Kelly and brother, Mitch. He knew she was attached to her family farm and the local community. Asking her to leave it all and live on the other side of the world was not going to work. She might like him as a friend, but it was too much to ask.

His stupid brain was awake now, trolling through thoughts about Kyla and their breakup, and Alanah and their hopeless future. Shut up! He needed sleep.

"Caleb?"

He cracked an eye open to see Alanah's beautiful face peering at him over the side of the truck. Sleeping in a truck cabin, no shower, no makeup. How did she emerge so fresh and lovely?

"Sorry. I didn't want to wake you, but it's eight o'clock. We need to have breakfast and clean up. I want to get to the embassy as soon as it opens."

"There's no hurry. The embassy isn't going anywhere." He rolled onto his back and stretched his shoulders and back.

"I know. I'm really sorry." Alanah had a small frown in her forehead. "I read online last night that it will take up to two business days for them to release an emergency passport. I don't want to waste any time getting the application in."

"What?" Caleb sat up. Two business days?

"I know you wanted to be back for the celebration, but that's today."

"I know what day it is." Whoops. That sounded sharp. But two days? Really?

"Do you have to open the shop or something tomorrow?" Alanah twisted her long golden-brown hair into a knot at the back of her head.

"No. I've got a couple of days off. It's just …"

Just what? It was just this was more time he had to spend with Alanah. Bittersweet. He wanted to cheer and swear all at once. He gave a half smile instead.

"It's fine, Alanah. I've got plenty of time. I'm sorry I'm such a bear this morning."

"You've just driven twenty-five hours and had six hours sleep in the back of a truck. It's understandable."

"Thanks." That was typical Alanah, considerate and forgiving. "This swag is comfortable to sleep in. I can't complain about that." He threw the canvas aside and got out of the truck bed.

"There's a bathroom behind the restaurants, with a shower."

"What are you saying?" He sniffed his armpits.

"Whatever, Caleb. I've had a shower. I'd go and buy breakfast, but unfortunately, I've run out of money."

He frowned.

"They stole my credit card as well."

"So have you cancelled it?"

"We did that before we did anything else."

"And have you ordered a replacement?"

"They're going to Fed Ex it to Trinity Lakes. It should be there when I get back. I'll pay you back then."

Caleb felt heat rise in his face. He hadn't meant to imply that he wasn't happy to pay for breakfast.

"It's all good, Alanah. I don't mind paying for a bit of food here and there."

"And petrol, unfortunately."

It was true. He'd paid for the gas so far and would for the rest of the journey. He didn't really expect her to pay him back. He reached for his wallet in his back pocket, opened it, and took out his credit card.

"Here. Can you order me the biggest breakfast they've got on the menu?"

"No food allergies to worry about?"

"No. And make sure you order what you want, too. I'll meet you inside shortly."

He did feel grimy. A shower would make him feel better about the day.

———

THREE BIO-SCANS, an interview, and pages of paperwork later, Alanah emerged from the interview room in the embassy and found Caleb dozing in the front seat of his truck.

"How did it go?" Caleb straightened and got out of the truck.

"About how I expected. The wheels of progress turn slowly in government departments."

"Same the world over, I guess."

Alanah smiled. "They'll send me a text when the passport is ready. They said they would try for the end of the day, or some-time tomorrow."

"Given we'd have to drive overnight again, we may as well wait until tomorrow."

Alanah peered at her watch. Eleven. It had only taken an hour to get an appointment, then another hour to go through the process. "I don't want to sit here in this car park all day. Should we do some sightseeing?"

"Ten steps in front of you." Caleb grinned. It was nice to see him relaxed at last. "I've searched the top spots and have two suggestions."

"Go on." Alanah waved her hand.

"Granville Island or Capilano Suspension Bridge."

"More information?"

"Granville island is a popular shopping precinct."

"I've already blown my budget and luggage weight limit. Besides, shopping isn't really my thing. What else?"

"Capilano Suspension Bridge. It's a simple suspension bridge crossing the Capilano River in the District of North Vancouver, British Columbia, Canada. The current bridge is 140 meters long and seventy meters above the river." He was reading from his phone.

"Is it in a park?"

Caleb nodded.

"Nature, and it won't cost us money. Let's do that."

"We can buy some lunch on the way, find a place to eat, then walk the bridge and some trails in the surrounding area. Hopefully by then the embassy will have sent you a text."

It was a good plan. The whole reason Alanah had gone to Canada in the first place was to do touristy things. She'd had a ball with Lucy. She would enjoy it just as much with Caleb. Possibly more, though she shouldn't let her mind go there.

As they drove out to the Capilano River Regional Park they stopped at a food market and purchased some picnic-style food. It was all so easy. Choosing stuff together was easy. Either Caleb was being extra agreeable to make up for his earlier grumps, or they got on well together. That was simple to figure out. They'd always got on well together in high school, and last night's cranky episode was probably attributed to driving many hours without sleep, not to mention a broken engagement.

Just thinking about Kyla sent stabs of guilt through Alanah. Was she the cause of the breakup? It seemed likely, yet Caleb was a man of integrity. Time to clear the air.

"I feel bad about Kyla." Caleb didn't respond. She cast a sideways glance in his direction. Mmm. His lips were pinched as if he was holding back.

"I'm sorry, Caleb. I know you must be hurting over it."

"That's the problem. I'm not hurting. I'm relieved, and that makes me feel bad. I should feel awful. I should be planning how to fix the problem, but all I can feel is: thank goodness it's over."

This was probably too much information. She shouldn't have pried. Should she say something?

"It's not your fault, Alanah. I think it would have come to this eventually anyway. Having you here has brought the problem to the surface earlier, which in the end, is better."

"I really am sorry."

"Don't worry about it. I'll talk to Kyla when we get back, but I've made up my mind. It wasn't meant to be. We wouldn't have been good together."

Right. Don't worry about it. A good plan ... or it would be if she didn't feel as if she was the other woman.

———

CALEB TOOK a deep breath of the clean forest air. This had been the right choice for the day. The Capilano River Suspension Bridge experience was more than just a suspended bridge high above the river ravine. It snaked through the treetops of the towering evergreens, the cedar-scented forest perfuming the air. There were seven suspended footbridges offering views of the forest floor, plus a cliff-top walk. It was magnificent, relaxing, and inspiring.

"Have you enjoyed the day?" Caleb asked Alanah as they hiked back to the parking lot.

"This is magnificent country. So different to where I live."

"Australia has a beauty of its own."

"Yeah, but this is so green and lush."

It was. From memory, the area where Alanah lived—the southern Flinders Ranges—was a combination of open plains, dry rocky creeks, and magnificent river red gums. And the blue mountain ranges. Not high enough to get snow, and in a region with a low rainfall, so no rivers. The creeks would run spasmodically during the wet season, but the countryside was characterized by the beauty of the dry. Hot and dry. And strangely, he missed it. Those had been some of the best years of his life.

He was suddenly knocked sideways as Alanah stumbled and fell into him. By instinct, he caught her and prevented her from falling. Lucky they weren't still suspended a hundred feet in the air. Then that thought evaporated from his mind. She was in his arms again, and he was right back where they'd left off eleven and a half years ago, lost in each other's gaze. His heart rate had accelerated. Sensible thought fled and he leaned in to kiss her. She didn't prevent him, but responded in kind, her arms going around his neck and accepting his lips as they softly explored hers. And there it was. The explosion of rockets and world-spinning passion. Everything he remembered from that time well in the past.

"Excuse me." A couple of hikers on the same trail waited to pass and the spell broke.

Caleb stood to one side but kept his arm around Alanah's waist. He smiled and gave a wink as the hikers passed by and moved on.

"I'm not sure that was wise," Alanah said.

"Wise?"

"You know. Stirring up something that has no future."

"Do we have to think of that now?" He wanted to behave like the teenage boy he'd been last time they'd kissed, but her sensible words challenged his emotionally charged actions.

"I love being with you, Caleb, I really do. If things were different, I wouldn't try to stop it from happening. But things are not different."

"Alanah. Please. Just for today." He pulled her close and wrapped his arms around her. She responded by resting her head on his shoulder. This was so right and so wrong all at the same time. As much as he relished holding Alanah, her words hammered away at his conscience like a woodpecker. Was this wise? It felt good, and his whole being wanted this and more, but was it wise?

"I can't do this, Caleb." Alanah pulled back. "I can't do this to Kyla."

Caleb didn't prevent her. She was right. For one thing, he needed to end things properly with Kyla, not leap into another relationship before having had a chance to discuss why the last one hadn't worked. And leaping into a relationship with Alanah … He let out a sigh.

"I know. I feel it too." She had stepped back but was still observing him.

"Like when we were kids?"

She nodded.

"I'm assuming the lush and green delights of North America aren't enough to entice you to move here?"

"I've thought about it—"

"Really?" What was that jolt of hope?

"It's beautiful country, and I love your family—"

"And me?"

"The jury is still out. Well, of course I love you, but do I love you enough to relocate to the other side of the world?"

"But you've thought about it? If there was a future for us, I mean?"

"I can't help thinking about it, though I know it is wrong. You are engaged to Kyla—"

"Was engaged."

"You had an argument and spoke in haste. I don't think that is so easily resolved."

Caleb shook his head. "If it isn't final yet, it will be. I've known for a long time that I made a mistake. It was wrong of me to let it drag out so long."

"Yes, well, I don't intend to be the one who has come between you."

"But what about …?" He waved his hand between them.

"It was wrong, wasn't it?" She sounded uncertain. He wanted to reassure her that it was perfectly right and beautiful, but he couldn't. He nodded instead.

"Let's keep our distance until we get back to Trinity Lakes. Really, Caleb. I think that's best."

His heart fell. All this time they had to spend together, and they had to pretend indifference. That was worse than not seeing her at all.

CHAPTER FOURTEEN

The text came at 4:35 p.m.

"Can we make it back to the embassy before it closes?" Alanah showed Caleb her phone.

"We're not that far away."

That horrible tension was back again. Hopes and joy had been squashed and they were both feeling it. As predicted, they rolled into the Australian Embassy car park at 4.50. The fact that a government department had done the job in half the estimated time lost its shine. Still, it was a relief to have the passport in her hand. She could get back to the USA. More importantly, she could get home.

"I think we should drive overnight again." Caleb spoke the minute Alanah got back in the truck.

"I'm worried about you, having driven so much."

"I'll be okay. Coffee is my friend."

Coffee? She was his friend too, but she wouldn't push the point. "If you're sure."

"We'll buy something to eat and then get back on the road," he said.

The plan was simple, but something about the way it was

delivered said he had withdrawn again. Ironic. That was what they had decided was the right thing to do, and now she was feeling hurt by it. Stupid emotions.

"The shortest route will take us through Seattle. Do you want to see anything there?"

At least he was talking to her.

"Do you recommend anything?"

Caleb shrugged. "We could see the Space Needle."

He wasn't keen. Neither was she, if she were honest. She just wanted to get back to Trinity Lakes and spend time with Sasha. After all, Sasha was the main reason Alanah came on this trip.

"Let's keep going. I want to get back to your folks."

"We'll get into Seattle around eight, eight thirty. There might be some fireworks somewhere."

Right. Independence Day. She'd forgotten.

"Let me search the internet to see if there's anything worth watching on our way."

Caleb nodded.

The Seattle fireworks show was scheduled to begin at ten. They would get there around eight. Did she want to spend a couple of hours in Seattle, seeing the city with Caleb, when they could just continue driving and probably get back to Trinity Lakes by midnight?

"What did you find out?"

"We have two choices. Stop in at Seattle and wait a couple of hours for the fireworks show, probably leave by ten thirty, and not get back to your place until two in the morning ..."

"Or?"

"Keep driving and get home by midnight." She glanced his way to gauge his reaction.

"I like the first choice, except..."

"Except its awkward us being together."

He nodded.

"But this is your one day in the year to celebrate independence." Even as the words came out of her mouth, she wondered if they could be taken in another way.

"We don't need to be awkward, Alanah. We've been friends for, how long?"

"I know. But …"

"But what? I'd like to see the fireworks. You can get a quick tour of Seattle, and we can share some time together."

"So long as we understand each other."

"Just friends." He sounded sure of himself.

"No kissing or hugging or handholding."

"None. I promise. I know you're right, so we'll keep a nice platonic distance."

Platonic distance. Sure. That was going to be easy. Not.

The miles passed, a stop at the border which wasn't too long a wait, then the two-hour drive to Seattle. Alanah wasn't a city girl. One city was pretty much like another in her opinion. Caleb pointed out a few interesting things as they drove to find a good spot to watch the fireworks.

Being a public holiday meant the roads were not so busy, but the parks and public areas in the city were crowded. It was a buzz and Alanah was glad Caleb was leading her. In the end, she amended the rules. It was easier holding his hand when making their way through the crowd to find a patch of lawn to sit on. It was nice, though she constantly told herself it was nothing of the kind—rather, it was expedient. Expedient handholding which ceased the moment they sat down on the grass.

"I guess this must be a good spot by the number of people trying to get a pozzie."

Alanah laughed at him. "That's so Aussie slang."

"I did learn something during my years in Australia." He grinned back at her.

"How often do you use Aussie slang and get strange looks?"

"I guess I've adopted some words into my vocabulary, and most people who know me are used to it by now."

"Tell me about Independence Day. What do I need to know?"

This time Caleb laughed. "Surely you've seen enough American television to get the idea."

"I know it has something to do with the signing of the Declaration of Independence, and a separation from England as a ruling power."

"That's it in a nutshell."

"What does it mean to you?"

Caleb frowned. "I didn't celebrate it as a kid, as we were in Australia celebrating Anzac Day and Australia Day. To be honest, it's an event so far in the past that I haven't really connected with what it has meant for me."

"Other than you have to play baseball instead of cricket."

"There's that." He laughed.

"There's a major controversy in Australia these days about Australia Day."

"What? Why?"

"It's the Indigenous day of mourning marked by the landing of the First Fleet. The First Nations People are calling it Invasion Day."

"Really?" Caleb sounded surprised.

"There's a growing consensus that we should celebrate Australia on another day that doesn't have such sorrowful connotations attached to it."

"Like Federation?"

"You know your Australian history."

"Except that's on January first. Which is already a public holiday."

"Correct, and you know how Aussies hate to let go of a public holiday."

"Sounds like a conundrum."

"It has taken the shine off Australia Day, which is a shame."

Alanah stretched and leaned back on her arms to gaze out over the water. It was a pleasant night, not too hot for the middle of summer, and she was enjoying the company, while pretending she wasn't.

Then the fireworks display began and filled the sky with the pop and crackle of explosives being let off, followed by the brilliant lively colors and sparkles. The crowd responded appropriately with clapping, oohs and aahs when something was particularly spectacular. The twenty-minute display was entertaining, and the night lost its excitement when the last of the fireworks had exploded into the sky. People immediately began to move, gathering blankets and picnic baskets.

"Well, I guess we'd best push on. I texted Mom to let her know we'd probably get in around two, two thirty." Caleb stood and held out his hands to help her stand. It was expedient. The crowds were thick and pushy, so Alanah threaded her arm through Caleb's for more expedience as they walked back to the truck.

"Are you sure you're okay to continue driving?" Alanah asked.

"We'll get a coffee from a drive-through on the way out, and I'm counting on you to keep me awake."

"I wish I could take a turn driving and help you out."

He squeezed her arm. "I value driving on the correct side of the road too much."

"Correct is all a matter of perspective. You know that."

He laughed again.

When they got to the truck, Alanah was reluctant to break the contact, but they had agreed. Platonic friendship. That was right. That was wise—until Caleb took her by the shoulders and gave her another kiss. Not too long, but it was enough. It was a rule-breaker.

"Caleb."

"I know. Not wise. I'm sorry."

"Except you're not."

"What? Sorry?"

Alanah nodded.

"No, I'm not sorry, but it won't happen again. I understand. It's just that you're so beautiful, and it's wonderful spending time with you."

"Caleb." She injected as much growl into her voice as she could muster.

"It's true."

"Thank you, that's nice of you to say so, but—"

"It's not wise."

"And that will be an end to it. Let's get you home and back to normal."

———

MOM HAD LEFT the outside light on, which would have annoyed the neighbors since they didn't roll into the driveway until nearly three. Alanah had tried to keep him awake for most of the drive, but she'd nodded off about forty-five minutes ago. She looked cute, snuggled into her jacket propped against the window.

"Alanah." He touched her shoulder lightly. "We're home."

She blinked her eyes open and stared blankly, confused for a moment until she oriented and sat up straight.

"Sorry, Caleb. I promised I'd keep you awake the whole way."

"I didn't have the heart to wake you. Anyway, we're here now. Let's get inside and get some sleep."

"Thank you again for coming to rescue me. I really appreciate it."

"I know." He smiled. "I was glad to spend the time with you, for old times' sake."

They got out of the car, Caleb lifted Alanah's luggage from the back of the truck, and they went inside. There was little point in tiptoeing as Mom was dozing on the sofa, waiting for them to arrive. Typical.

"You shouldn't have waited up," Caleb said as he kissed his mother's cheek.

"I wouldn't have slept until I knew you were home and safe."

Alanah smiled. "My mum is the same. She's fine if she's not expecting me, but she won't sleep if I've said I'll be home that night."

"It's a mother thing. You two will understand one day."

"Mom." So awkward.

"I meant when you become parents."

From bad to worse. He gave his best frown.

"When you and Kyla become parents. Goodness, Caleb. You're so sensitive."

Was it worth going into it at this time of night?

"I'll hit the hay," Alanah said. A quick extraction from Mom's clumsy faux pax. "Should I use the same room as before?"

"I've set up a cot in Sasha's room. I'm surprised she hasn't woken up."

Alanah lifted her heavy suitcase and headed to the staircase.

"I'll carry it upstairs for you, if you like." This was a good opportunity to end the awkward conversation with Mom. There would be time enough later to go into the details regarding his relationship with Kyla.

"You should tell her." Thankfully, Alanah used a discreet tone as they got to the landing.

"I will. I need to talk to Kyla first. It's too up in the air at the moment and I need to clear the air with her."

"I'm glad you're going to talk to her. She must feel awful about what's happened."

So like Alanah. Thinking about how someone else was feeling rather than how she felt.

"Goodnight, Caleb." She quietly pushed open Sasha's bedroom door—no pause to allow a hug or kiss to develop. Wise woman.

ALANAH CLOSED the door quietly behind her. What was Mrs. Kennedy on about? The way she put it, it sounded like she was talking about her and Caleb being parents. It would be embarrassing, except it was a beautiful idea. An impossible, beautiful idea.

Sasha's room was not completely dark. She'd left a small plug-in wall light on which gave a warm ambiance to the room. Sasha stirred and turned over.

"You're back at last." The sleep in her voice didn't diminish Sasha's evident joy.

"I missed you."

Sasha sat up. "What time is it?"

"After three."

"Are you tired?"

"Bushed, but I'm tempted to lie awake and talk about all the things we'd planned to talk about."

"I'll let you sleep if you want, but could you give me three or four dot points for me to ponder."

Three or four dot points. So much had happened that it was not easily condensed. Besides, there was only one point swirling around and around in her brain. Caleb had kissed her. She had kissed him. What on earth had she been thinking?

"How did you get along with Lucy?"

"Loved it. We had such a good time. The only downer was that you weren't there."

"I know, right. I got to go back and forth to the hospital for treatment and PT. Not what I'd had in mind."

"I hope you and Derek get to go to some of these places on your honeymoon."

"Forget it. We've booked to go to the Caribbean. Next time you come we'll do a revisit."

Next time. Would she ever leave home and do that horrible

long-haul flight again? She loved Sasha, but not sure she loved her that much.

"How did you get along with Caleb?"

"What?" Her attention was jerked back.

"Caleb. How did you get along with him the last couple of days?"

What was she supposed to say? She opened her suitcase and rifled around for her pjs.

"Alanah?"

"Yes, Sasha?" Alanah began to strip off her t-shirt in the dim light. Sasha turned the other way, but her connection to the conversation didn't lessen.

"What aren't you telling me?"

How could she tell?

"Alanah?"

"We kissed, all right. I didn't mean to, but it happened."

The silence that descended was unnerving.

"He broke up with Kyla, and I felt really bad, and I told him how bad I felt, and we just got close, you know when you're traveling together, and I told him it wasn't wise."

"Alanah. Take a breath."

Alanah stopped and stared in the dim light at her friend, who by this time, was sitting up, staring right back at her.

"I feel terrible."

"Really?"

"No. It felt wonderful, but it was wrong. He'd only just broken up with Kyla earlier in the day. And even then, he shouldn't … we shouldn't …"

"Calm down, Alanah. Take a breath."

Good advice. Deep breath in. Hold. Slow release. Put on the pajamas.

Sasha didn't speak while Alanah readied for bed, just reviewed her mobile phone giving Alanah some privacy to change. Only when Alanah was settled on the fold-out bed did Sasha speak again.

"She came over and spent the evening with us for the fireworks."

"What? Who?"

"Kyla. She came over in the late afternoon, a bag of snacks in hand, and said she'd love to watch the fireworks with us, and maybe catch Caleb when he got home."

"How did she seem?"

"Happy. Schmoozing all over us like we're family."

"Well, you are the intended in-laws."

"I thought you said they broke up."

"That's what Caleb told me when he picked me up. Apparently she gave him an ultimatum."

"And he chose you."

"Sasha, stop. We're not going there."

"But you kissed him."

The conversation stalled. That was the material point. She hadn't been angry with Caleb when he'd kissed her. She'd joined in with enthusiasm—then thought better of it.

"This is such a mess, Sash. I feel like I've made Caleb cheat on Kyla."

"Well ..."

Sasha paused. What was she thinking? She was supposed to be offering reassurance at this point.

"I have, haven't I? I've caused him to cheat on Kyla."

"Well ... I'm sure you didn't mean to."

"I didn't. But I enjoyed it too much. I lost my mind. Oh, Sasha. What am I going to do? Should I get an early flight home?"

"Cut that out! You came here for me. To be my chief bridesmaid. I will not have my brother and his unsuitable girlfriend chasing you away before I've had my time with you."

Alanah swallowed the lump that had risen in her throat. She

wanted to spend time with Sasha too. Do all the wedding shopping, and help get everything ready, and enjoy her time away from her usual life.

"Let's just go to sleep now, and we'll see how the dust settles tomorrow."

Sasha leaned over and switched off the small wall light, and Alanah could hear her settling down into bed.

"It will be all right, Alanah. Don't get yourself into a knot over it. We'll sort it out tomorrow."

Easy for Sasha to say.

CHAPTER FIFTEEN

Tuesday. Caleb glanced at his watch. Seeing it was after eleven, he jolted fully awake. Sure, he hadn't got to sleep until after three thirty, but half the day was gone. Was he supposed to open the shop or not? It was the day after the Fourth of July, when people were still in vacation mode. Most of the music students were all on summer break, so they wouldn't be in. There were a handful of adult students, and they wouldn't be in until late afternoon. It had been busy prior to the parade. He couldn't remember if he'd told Elaine he would be back today or not. She had probably guessed by now, since it was so late.

He typed a text to let her know he'd decided to take the day off, apologized, and pressed send. He wanted to see Kyla today, to finally sort out the end to their relationship. Another text and he got out of bed. What was Alanah doing today? *Don't go there.* She was here to spend time with Sasha. They'd discussed what was wise. Caleb constantly thinking about her was not in the plan.

The ping of his phone told him someone had replied. Elaine. No problem. She wasn't expecting to be busy anyway.

The only problem was another day without pay. Lucky he was still freeloading at his parents' house. His brain was full of fuzz, the product of not enough sleep, but his gut was churning. Alanah was in the house, and he was trying to suppress the urge to go find her. More importantly, he didn't imagine the conversation with Kyla was going to be easy. Sleep deprived or not, he had to face her and talk things through properly.

"What are your plans for the day?" Mom was also on school vacation and baking in the kitchen. Whatever it was, it smelled great.

"I've got to go spend some time with Kyla."

"Right. She was disappointed not to catch you last night."

"Last night? Did she call?"

"No, she came over and spent the evening with us. Even came down to the lake to watch the fireworks display."

What was she doing? Anxiety reached out and grabbed him by the throat. Kyla had said it was over. Based on that, he'd stepped way over the line with Alanah. And it was over with Kyla. He wasn't going to be reigniting anything.

"How did she seem?" Caleb asked as he put a savory bite, hot off the cookie sheet, into his mouth.

"She was fine. Happy even. In fact, she seemed pleased to be here. I don't recall her ever being so congenial on past visits."

A rock sunk in Caleb's stomach. What was she playing at? Kyla had only ever come to visit his family with the barest amount of civility. He wouldn't say it out loud, but this seemed like she was playing his family to get to him.

He pointed to the tray of egg and bacon pastry bites. "These things are brilliant. Are they for a special purpose?"

"It's summer break. I have time to bake, so I'm baking."

"I can have more?"

"Help yourself."

He didn't have to be told twice.

"Sasha and Alanah are out for brunch, and planning to go to the mall in Walla Walla after."

Caleb didn't reply, just kept eating his mother's excellent breakfast snack.

"Will you go with them?"

He'd love nothing better, but it wasn't going to happen. He shook his head. "No, I've got to catch up with Kyla today. I've got some students later in the afternoon, and back to work tomorrow."

"I was surprised you didn't get Kyla to go with you on your rescue trip. Did you ask her?"

He shook his head. He didn't really want to talk about this yet.

"Was she okay with it when you told her?"

Caleb sucked in a deep breath.

"Caleb?" She was like a dog at a bone—she wasn't going to let this go.

"We broke up," he said.

"When?"

"When she discovered I'd gone to Canada without her."

"Oh, Caleb. You should have discussed it with her."

"Why?"

"Because she's your fiancée. How do you think she felt when she found out?"

"Whose side are you on?"

"I'm on the side of reconciliation and marital harmony."

"We're not getting married. It's finished."

Mom had her teacher glare on—the one that could subdue a class of raucous fifteen-year-olds without a word.

"I'm not going to reconcile. Kyla and I would not be happy."

"You can't just jump in and out of relationships based on emotional highs and lows."

"I know that, Mom. Why do you think I persisted with her for so long?"

"What do you mean?"

"I mean she's been insecure, controlling, demanding, and unkind to people I hold dear ever since we got engaged."

"She wasn't like this before?"

"Not that I'd noticed. But it became apparent that she planned to arrange my life to suit her, and it didn't include you or any of my friends."

"You mean Alanah?"

"She flared worse than ever when Alanah arrived, but the controlling and demanding behavior has been there the whole time."

Mom went quiet. She was thinking this through.

Caleb's phone pinged and he checked it. Kyla.

Let's have lunch together. I missed you. Meet at Becky's Coffee Cart? Her light-hearted invitation was accompanied by a love heart and a kissing emoji. It was as if Sunday morning's conversation had never happened. How was he going to deal with this?

"Kyla?" Mom was still watching him.

"Apparently her ultimatum didn't mean what I thought she meant."

"Ultimatum?"

"She wanted me to leave Alanah stranded—either I came back, or the relationship was over. I've been feeling it a while, and it was easy to choose. I care about Alanah."

"Caleb. You haven't started anything with Alanah?" By Mom's tone he could tell she would not approve. "Caleb."

"I haven't started anything that wasn't already there."

"Meaning?"

"Meaning I was in love with her in high school, we started something at our graduation, but then you brought us all back here to Trinity Lakes."

"I didn't know that."

"Yeah, well …"

"I'm so sorry. You must have been heartbroken."

"Understatement." Of the decade.

"But why didn't you and Alanah keep the relationship going?"

"It wasn't just long distance. It was the other side of the planet. She's attached to her family and home, and I'm attached to my family."

"Has anything changed since she arrived?"

"No. We can't go anywhere with it. She'll go home after the wedding."

"Well, that's good—I think. At the moment, you've got to talk to Kyla and sort that out."

"I'm not going to go on with it."

"Nevertheless, you need to give her the benefit of talking to you face to face."

"I know. She's asked me out to lunch. I'd better get ready to go meet her."

"I'll pray for you—for wisdom."

"Thanks, Mom. I could use a truckload of wisdom right now."

He stood from the table just as the front door opened. The girls were back, so it was time for him to exit.

———

BECKY'S COFFEE CART was set up in a park not far from the lake, with scattered cafe tables set up around. Caleb didn't feel like eating—having stuffed ten of Mom's delicious bites into his mouth. Kyla had said lunch, but Becky Gilbertson served mainly coffee and muffins or cookies. He didn't want to appear unprepared, so he stopped in at the Bellbird Cafe and grabbed some lunch food.

The advantage of being in an open-air location was the beautiful fresh air and sunshine. There were a few people down at the lake, but not many around the coffee cart, so they would have some privacy. Kyla pulled her car next to his truck in the parking lot a few minutes after he'd cut his engine.

How was this going to play out? She'd been furious last time they'd spoken. He'd been furious. And since then ...

"I've missed you." Kyla threw her arms around his neck and kissed him enthusiastically. He lifted his arms about her waist, but it was half-hearted. Surely she could tell he was not responding.

"Hope you had a good time with your friend."

"Are you talking about Alanah?"

"Sure. You went to rescue her, right?"

"Kyla." He pushed back from her. "You gave me an ultimatum. Choose me or choose Alanah. Remember?"

She moved back in, putting her arms around his waist and laying her head on his shoulder.

"You're here, aren't you? Obviously you've chosen me, your promised wife."

He felt like a heel, but he had to put distance between them. "I took you at your word, Kyla. You have been jealous, demanding, and controlling ever since Alanah arrived, and I'm not happy about it."

"I know. I'm sorry. I should have been more understanding. You were close to her in high school. I understand."

"Understand?" What was she doing?

"It was unfair of me to be so demanding. I just hated the thought of losing you."

"Well, I'm sorry to say, but you have lost me. You lost me some time ago, but I only got the chance to put it into words when you called me."

"You don't mean that, Caleb. We're good together. We'll make a great team when we're married."

Could he do it? Could he push back against this sudden show of affection and kind understanding? It was fake. He knew it was fake. She was manipulating him again.

"Let's just have lunch and after a walk down to the lake, I'm sure you'll feel better about it."

Should he? Alanah was flying home soon. Would Kyla settle into something amiable? But then, even if she did, he'd known from the beginning that she didn't ignite the feelings in him that he knew were possible.

"Come on, Caleb. Let's grab one of the tables and sit down."

The choice was upon him. He either made his feelings plain right here, right now, or he caved and committed to her for the rest of his life. His mother would lecture him on allowing his feelings to rule, and she was probably right. But there was a whole lot more to it than emotions. He had seen a side of Kyla that disturbed him, something that made him cringe to think he would be bound to her for life.

"Kyla, wait."

This was not going to be easy, but it had to be done. Kyla was not the woman for him.

———

ALANAH WAS EXHAUSTED. Luckily, so was Sasha, after having crutched from store to store in search of bridesmaid's dresses and other accessories. Hair combs, shoes, wedding guest gifts. Thankfully, Mr. Kennedy had driven them to Walla Walla, and Mrs. Kennedy had picked them up. Alanah wanted to be useful and had driven around a couple of streets in Trinity Lakes, but it had terrified her because her brain wanted her to drive on the left side of the road—and she didn't even want to talk about left hand turns. Better she remain a passenger. Sasha's parents were on summer break and didn't seem to mind running around after them.

When they got inside the Kennedy home, Sasha got herself up the stairs and proclaimed she was taking a nap for a week. Alanah was tempted to join her but wanted a cold drink first.

The summer weather wasn't as hot and dry as she was used to in Australia. It was a pleasant twenty-nine degrees Celsius. Of course, she'd had to Google the temperature as the locals talked in Fahrenheit. Apparently today was eighty-five degrees. She was used to week-long heat waves where the mercury would climb well over forty degrees—one hundred Fahrenheit. Twenty-nine was much easier to handle.

Marianne had gone outside to read on the deck, and Caleb's dad had gone into his den, probably to read also. It was strange having a quiet and easy summer. In Australia, summer break included the Christmas madness as well as all the end-of-year parties.

Alanah poured herself a tall glass of water. They had iced tea, but it wasn't something she'd drunk before. It was too sweet for her liking. Water would do the job. She was just putting her glass back in the sink when she heard voices in the living room —Caleb and his mother. She must have come back inside.

"I broke it off for good." Caleb sounded relieved.

"Are you sure?" Marianne, not so much.

"It wouldn't have worked."

"How did she take it?"

"She pretended I was joking and tried to sweet-talk me back, but I couldn't."

"Was this because of Alanah?"

"No."

"Really?"

"No, Mom. There's no future for me and Alanah. Besides, I wanted Kyla to understand I was breaking up with her because of us, not because of a doomed love affair from the past."

Doomed love affair. It was true, but it hurt to hear it said out loud.

"What happened after you told her?" Marianne pushed.

"She dropped the act and threw out some fairly low accusations."

"Like?"

"It doesn't matter." Caleb sounded discouraged and Alanah wanted to join them for the discussion.

"Because they're not true?" There was concern in Marianne's tone.

Caleb didn't answer. The accusations could be true, and that was the trouble. What would Caleb say?

"What did she say?" Marianne sounded determined to get to the bottom of it.

"She thinks I hooked up with Alanah and that's why I broke up with her."

"Did you? Did you hook up with Alanah?" Alanah could imagine Marianne using air quotes around the slang term.

"Not really."

"Either you did or you didn't."

"I'm a little offended that you'd believe I would break up with my fiancée in the morning and sleep with my old girlfriend in the evening."

"Then what did you do with your old girlfriend in the evening?"

"We kissed a couple of times. That's it. Alanah is more sensible than me and put a stop to anything going forward."

"I hope you weren't inappropriate with her."

"Yes, it was inappropriate to be getting so close to a woman right on the heels of a breakup, but I didn't force myself on her, if that's what you mean. Alanah still feels the same about me as I do her."

"You're sure about that?"

"That's what she told me."

"And yet …?"

"And yet Australia and America are still an ocean apart. I can't ask her to give up her home and family. This is exactly where we were eleven and a half years ago."

"I'm sorry, Caleb. This is a difficult time for you."

"Well, you can make it easier if you help me avoid both Alanah and Kyla. I need to get my head sorted."

"You need to get your heart sorted." There was empathy in Marianne's tone.

The conversation ended with what sounded like a hug. Alanah shouldn't have been listening. But how could she get from here to the staircase without them seeing her? She'd have to leave through the laundry door, which meant her nap wasn't going to happen. Probably just as well, since there was no way she could sleep now.

So the next few weeks would be Operation Avoid Caleb.

Why did that hurt so much?

CHAPTER SIXTEEN

Caleb lifted his guitar from the back of his truck and headed toward the front entrance of the church building. It was great to have an excuse to be out of the house. A jam session with a few of the church musicians was just what he needed to take his mind off everything.

"Hey, mate." Alex greeted Caleb as he walked in the door. "Missed you at the fireworks the other night."

"I was sent on a rescue mission."

"Really? Who and where?"

"Sasha's friend from Australia was touring in Canada and had her passport and credit cards stolen."

"Wow. Did she get that sorted out?"

"After a thirty-hour round car trip, and not a lot of sleep."

"Hi, Caleb." Alex's cousin, Beau joined them. "You look tired."

Good observation. He was still recovering from the trip and wasn't sleeping well with all the emotional upheaval going on. Kyla's accusations had been destructive, made worse because they held a seed of truth. He shouldn't have proposed to her in the first place, and he certainly shouldn't have kissed Alanah.

"Let's play some music." He could use the focus that came with keeping in rhythm with the other musicians.

He set up his guitar while the others got their instruments ready. Beau worked the sound desk to mix them to a suitable sound. It was great having Alex part of the group, given his professional experience.

After twenty minutes of rehearsing together, the lyrics and spirit of the songs began to do their work. There was nothing like allowing himself to be wrapped in the sound of worship to God, and the gentle comfort and strength that resulted. This was exactly what he needed.

He opened his eyes when the others suddenly stopped playing mid-song. The pastor had entered and was waiting, his focus directly on Caleb.

"Hi, Pastor Dean."

"Could you all spare Caleb for a bit?" The pastor's words sounded like a question, but his tone was more like a command. This felt like a trip to the principal's office and Caleb's mouth went dry. What was wrong?

"See you after," Alex called as Caleb left the stage and followed the pastor from the sanctuary. Caleb lifted his hand and tried a reassuring smile which, given his current state of heart, must have seemed weak. The expression of concern on Alex's face told him all he needed to know.

"Tell me about you and Kyla." Pastor Dean had hardly sat down before he began his interrogation—and it truly seemed like an interrogation.

"We've broken up." Really, was this any of his business?

"Kyla told me you had cheated on her with the girl from Australia, but that she wants to forgive you and restore the relationship."

Kyla would not let this go. Caleb's anger flared.

"My breaking up with Kyla had nothing to do with my friend from Australia."

"So you didn't sleep with her?"

A rocket fired in his gut. "Who—? Actually, cancel that question. I haven't slept with *anyone*. As I'm sure you're aware, I hold to the traditional Christian moral values, and I resent that you're even asking me."

"Kyla believes that you were unfaithful to her."

"I ended my relationship with Kyla after she tried to blackmail me with an ultimatum."

"So nothing happened with the Australian girl?"

"Her name is Alanah, and we are old friends from when we were kids."

The pastor didn't say anything, but raised his eyebrows, an expression that was as powerful in demanding an answer as if he'd asked aloud.

"I kissed Alanah a couple of times, but only after Kyla and I had broken up."

"That's not how Kyla sees it."

"Well, I've finished it with her completely now, so it isn't really any of her business."

The pastor sucked in a deep breath, his mouth in a grim line.

"I think it's unfair that this has come to your office at all, and that you see it as your duty to grill me on my private life." Caleb probably should have been more respectful, but this seemed like a massive intrusion.

"You are one of our youth leaders, Caleb, and on our worship team. I'm sure you understand that as senior pastor I need to make sure that those who are influencing our young people are behaving as proper role models."

"Fine." Caleb couldn't help the irritation that had crept into his tone.

"Fine?" Pastor Dean's eyebrows nearly reached his hairline now.

"You know it all, and if you think it's inappropriate, I'll happily stand down."

"Good."

"What?"

"I think that is the best idea for the time being."

"You think I should stop helping with youth?"

"And the worship team."

"Because I kissed an old friend?"

"Because you are in a state of agitation, and your relationship with Kyla is in tatters."

"My relationship with Kyla is done. Over. Finished. I should've ended it long before. There will be no reconciliation."

"Are you sure? You and she would have made a great ministry team."

"That's a nice sentiment, Pastor Dean, and possibly why I'm in this hole to start with."

"What do you mean by that?" Pastor Dean sounded defensive.

"One of the reasons I asked Kyla to marry me in the first place was because of this ..." He waved his hand around the office. "This expectation."

"What expectation, Caleb? And I think you should watch your tone."

He should. He was fired up. He took a deep breath. "I was always being reminded that Kyla would make a great pastor's wife. That we would work well together in ministry."

"That is true."

"Is it? From where I stand, it looks more like ambition and vying for a position. I shouldn't have asked her to marry me in the first place. Our friendship was okay, but it didn't have what's needed for a strong marriage. I shouldn't have asked her."

"Well, you did ask her, and I'm not happy knowing you've established this bond and are so willing to toss it aside. And there's the matter of cheating on her."

Caleb ground his teeth. "If you are going to stand people

down because they are not acting as proper role models, I hope your next call will be to Kyla."

"Why?"

"Because she is controlling, manipulative, demanding, insecure, jealous—"

Pastor Dean held up his hand. "Those are fairly strong accusations, Caleb."

This time Caleb remained silent, rolling his lips tightly together.

"All right. This is turning into a mess. I will talk to Kyla and perhaps you can come in together."

"No!" Caleb stood up. "I don't want anything more to do with her. She might present all spiritual and enthusiastic, but there is another side to her you haven't seen."

Pastor Dean also stood.

"All right, Caleb. I can see this is a highly volatile situation for you. It's best if you step down from the youth and music teams for a while. Perhaps we can talk about this later."

How had Kyla coerced the pastor, of all people, to believe her side of the story? He stormed out the door without another word. He'd have gone straight to his truck to drive around and blow off steam, but he still had to retrieve his guitar.

"Hey, mate." Alex met him in the foyer. "You don't look so good."

"I'm furious."

"Do you want to talk about it?"

Caleb nodded. He couldn't go back home. Imagine having to tell this whole story to his parents again, and he dreaded seeing Alanah. It was too much.

———

"CALEB, THAT'S A MESS, MATE." Alex's words were the understatement of the year.

"There's nothing I can do about it." Caleb appreciated having the opportunity to vent his frustration to someone he trusted.

"What about Alanah?"

"It's not going to happen. I shouldn't have allowed her to get so close to me again."

"But she's staying at your folks place until Sasha gets married?"

"Another eight weeks." Eight weeks of torture.

"You're welcome to crash here if you like."

Caleb surveyed the small living area. Alex already had a housemate and his cousin, Beau, and it wasn't a big place.

"Would it be okay if I took the sofa for tonight, at least? I'll sort something out tomorrow."

"Sure."

Alex found a scruffy sheet and a sad pillow and threw them on the sofa.

"On second thought, I have my swag in the back of my truck."

"You have a swag?" Alex's eyes lit. "Like an Aussie swag?"

"They sell them over here now in camping stores."

"Mate, I didn't know that. I'll have to get one."

"I'll get mine and set it up on the floor. Save messing up your linen."

Not that Alex's linen was pristine to start with. It had already seen hard days, by the look of it.

The other guys had turned in for the night, but Caleb was still agitated. He sent a text to his parents to let them know he wouldn't be home. Mom sent back a concerned question.

I'll tell you about it later. Just spending some time with a mate on the worship team.

Mom meant well, but sometimes he would prefer to be able to just stew on things on his own.

By the time Beau got up for work at five, Caleb had only been asleep about two hours. This sleep deprivation thing was wearing his fuse down to almost nothing. No wonder he'd been so short with Pastor Dean.

The day had begun and the others slowly emerged, getting ready for their day jobs. Caleb wasn't expected in at the music store until ten, but trying to grab a bit more sleep was impossible with the others coming in and out of the main living area.

Eventually he got up and took a cold shower to shock him into alertness. When he emerged, the house was clear. Time to think. He needed to keep his distance from Alanah for a while. That meant staying away from home. Alex had said he was welcome to stay as long as he liked, but this wasn't workable. Caleb pulled out his cell phone and sent a text to Jason.

You up for a housemate for a few weeks?

He waited. Jason wouldn't be at work yet, but it was a long shot. Jason wasn't the most easygoing friend he had, but he was a genuine guy, and would help him out.

The message pinged back.
Sure. What's up?

Long story. I'll fill you in after work.

Since you're coming, you can cook.
Typical Jason. He wasn't afraid to ask someone else to cook. Fair's fair. Jason was letting him stay.

Now to text Mom and let her know. On the other hand, knowing Mom's desperation for details, it would be easier for him to call. It would not be a short call.

CHAPTER SEVENTEEN

Alanah hadn't seen Caleb for four days. It was a relief, wasn't it? But she couldn't help missing him. When was he coming home? Marianne didn't offer any information, and neither did his dad.

"I haven't seen Caleb in a while." Just a harmless statement. Sasha might have some insight.

"He's moved out until after the wedding."

"What?" A spike of hurt sliced her inside. "Is he avoiding me?"

"I thought you said this was best. You two can't keep seeing each other, pining away for a relationship that's never going to happen."

"I know, but ..." But what? She loved Caleb. That was the trouble. But apparently, so did Kyla. What a shemozzle. He was right. It was best they didn't see each other anymore.

"Are you sure you couldn't bring yourself to move here permanently?" Sasha's tone was sad and pleading.

"I love you, Sash, and your whole family ..."

"Especially Caleb."

She shook her head. She couldn't acknowledge that Caleb

meant anything more to her than the rest of the family. It was dangerous for her emotional state.

"But I couldn't sever myself from home. It's a big deal."

Sasha nodded. "I'm sorry. I shouldn't have asked. I know how far away Booleroo Whim is from Trinity Lakes, and I know how different living there is from living here. It was an adventure for us."

"Exactly, and if I had to come here forever, it wouldn't be an exciting adventure. It would be the loss of my family and home."

"I get it. I'm sorry."

"Me too."

Sasha pushed back from the breakfast table.

"Well, we have more shopping and wedding planning to do. Are you up for it?"

Alanah got up as well. Of course she was up for it. That was why she'd come, and she had lost enough time with Sasha already. She was going to enjoy every last minute with Sasha Kennedy before she became Mrs. Derek Beale.

"When will you be free of crutches?"

"I'm hoping I can swap to a moon boot after this week's hospital visit."

"And hopefully be free for your wedding shoes in time."

"Given how wobbly I feel on my feet, I might just go for white sneakers."

Alanah laughed.

"We could get some ribbon and bling them up a bit."

"If you're wearing sneakers, then so am I. I hate heels."

"You're such a country girl."

"I am, and that's not likely to change."

Sasha gave a sad smile. "I know, Lani. I know."

———

IT WAS AMAZING how time flew and moved like a glacier at the same time. Caleb's days and nights away from home—away from seeing Alanah—were achingly slow. But it was now only a few days until the wedding, which meant Alanah would be leaving Trinity Lakes for good.

"Mate, you're like a lovesick pup." Jason threw the pizza box into the trash. "Why don't you just ask her to marry you?"

"We've been over this. And besides, you of all people should understand. Isn't your Mom an Aussie? She must have found it difficult having to leave and live in the States."

"Yeah. It didn't end well."

"I'll get over Alanah. Eventually. Having you let me stay at your place has really helped. Thanks, mate."

"You can't stay here forever, you know."

"Yeah, I get it. Selena wouldn't be happy with me around as a third wheel."

"Are you going to live back with your folks once Alanah leaves?"

Caleb paused. He'd thought about it long and hard. It was way past time to move out. If he'd married Kyla, he would have organized a place and moved out sooner rather than later. But that was over—thank the Lord. Even though he'd spent the last two months battling church gossip and dark glares from people who thought they knew everything. He'd put up with it. He'd determined to be the bigger man and did his best not to sink to Kyla's level. He refused to spread more gossip about Kyla, despite his lingering anger. The Lord, and people close to him, knew the truth of things, and that was the only thing that mattered.

But would he move out?

"Let's see what happens after Sasha and Derek settle in their new place," Caleb said.

"Have you got your suit sorted for the wedding?" Jason asked.

"Sasha has sorted it, but I have to make sure it fits."

"Better get on it. You don't want to be the only one who isn't dressed properly."

Caleb smiled. He would get it sorted. Sasha had texted him numerous times in the last few days, asking when he was going to try it on. He'd been avoiding it. Derek was having him as one of the groomsmen. Thank goodness he wasn't best man, as then he would have had to partner with Alanah.

Alanah. Always Alanah. He'd just said he would get over her eventually. How long did it take for eventually?

His phone pinged. Sasha.

I'm coming around tomorrow and taking you to get that suit fitted. You're driving me crazy, Caleb.

"She's stressed." Jason had glanced at the text as he was sitting next to Caleb on the couch. "Weddings bring a lot of stress, so I'm told."

Caleb nodded and prepared to return the text.

I'm going in tomorrow. I'll be ready.

You'd better be. BTW don't forget to dress nicely for the rehearsal dinner tomorrow night.

What did she mean by nicely? "What's your advice here?" He showed the text to Jason.

"Nicely. Don't wear jeans and a t-shirt. Get a haircut, and have a shower before you go."

"You make me sound like I've deteriorated into a homeless person."

"I've seen you looking better."

"Yeah, well …"

"You're depressed, I suppose. But you'll need to get your butt into gear. This is your sister's wedding. Make an effort, man."

Caleb sighed. He would make an effort for Alanah's sake.

Wait.

Did he just think Alanah?

Sasha.

MEREDITH RESCE

This was for Sasha's sake. His twin sister was getting married, and he needed to get a grip.

———

THE HOUSE HAD BEEN a buzz of energy since five-thirty in the morning.

"Are you excited?"

Alanah was surprised by Sasha's question. This was Sasha's big day, not hers. Was she excited? They had already started the beautification process, but there was nothing more to be done until the hairdresser arrived.

"The question is, are *you* excited?" Actually, that was a silly question. Her best friend was almost floating around the house. She'd had moments of stress, like when Caleb had left it until the last minute to make sure his suit fitted, but on the whole, the Kennedy girls were an organizational machine, and the day appeared to be on schedule.

"I can't wait."

"To be married?"

Sasha gave her a smile with a waggle of eyebrows.

Alanah smiled back, but it belied how she felt. Sasha would go off on her honeymoon with the man she loved, and Alanah would board her flight back to Adelaide via Los Angeles and Sydney. In only two days she would leave the Kennedys, and one Kennedy in particular. One she wished she didn't have to leave behind.

Could she stay? That question had hounded her for all the weeks leading up to the wedding, especially after the rehearsal dinner two nights ago. Caleb had looked devastatingly handsome in his casual grey sports jacket and button-down blue checked shirt. He'd been polite, but distant. She hadn't encouraged him, though three times she'd caught him staring at her across the room—or had he caught her staring at him? Perhaps they'd been staring at each other. Sasha would likely have called her out, but she was too caught up with her own happy ever after. As she should be.

"It's time for breakfast." Marianne called up the stairs.

"How does she think I'm going to be able to eat?" Sasha was wrapped in her silk dressing gown, her wet hair combed back into a knot on the back of her head.

"I don't want you fainting in the middle of the ceremony because your blood sugar level is low. We're eating."

"Yes, ma'am." Sasha followed Alanah downstairs.

The whole Kennedy clan sat around the table for Sasha's last breakfast as a Kennedy, except Caleb. Two more days. Alanah stifled the sigh that had built in her heart. She needed to be alert and focused on Sasha.

They'd all sat down to a full breakfast—fruit, yoghurt, waffles, crispy bacon, and syrup. Alanah was getting used to it after these past months, though she doubted she'd start pouring maple syrup on her bacon once she got back home. There were limits.

James Kennedy glanced at his watch. Why wasn't he praying? Sasha may not have been hungry, but Alanah was famished.

"What time did Caleb say he was getting here?" James asked his wife.

"He'll be here in a minute," Marianne replied.

"He's always late." Alanah studied Lucy as she complained about her brother.

Late? Were they expecting Caleb? Alanah cast a glare she hoped communicated horror in Sasha's direction. Sasha shrugged, obviously understanding.

"He's my twin brother, Lani. This is our last breakfast all together as a family, and I wanted him here."

"You could have warned me." Alanah was ultra-aware of her wet messy hair, and the fact that she was still in a dressing

169

gown. No make-up yet. She didn't want Caleb to see her in this bedraggled state.

"You look fine." Sasha got it. She always got it.

"Perhaps I'll go upstairs and let your family enjoy the time together without outsiders."

"Don't be silly. You're not an outsider. You're family."

Lucy leaned into the conversation. "I get it, Alanah. If you feel more comfortable, you could go upstairs."

She was just about to push back from the table when the back door opened, and Caleb came in. He was dressed in running shorts and t-shirt, and his hair was mussed. His beautification process obviously hadn't started yet. But he didn't need it. This image was ... gorgeous. It was killing her. His eyes landed on her first, and Alanah could feel the blood rising in her face. Why didn't he look at his beloved twin sister? She was the bride. She was the one about to leave and set up home with her new husband.

"Good, you're here." The middle brother, Matt was eyeing the food. "Hurry up. We haven't got all day."

Caleb pulled out a chair in the place left for him, right opposite Alanah. The temptation to just sit and stare was overwhelming. Would it be obvious when the whole Kennedy family had descended into loud talking—after James' prayer, of course—and helping themselves to the array of breakfast foods laid out on the table? Before she could tear her eyes away, Caleb glanced up and gave her a smile. There was nothing she could say. Two days and she would be gone. This was hard.

"What time are you going to Derek's to get ready?" Sasha interrupted the silent connection, directing her question to Caleb.

"Straight after breakfast. I wouldn't want to get in the way of you girls."

"I'm coming with you." Matt stuffed another bite of waffle in his mouth and didn't finish chewing before he continued. "Derek won't mind if I get ready at his house, will he, Sash?"

"Why don't you get ready here?"

"Too much female fussing."

"You're driving one of the cars," Marianne said to her younger son. "You'd better be back on time."

"What's the deadline?" Matt didn't appear to be overly worried.

"One o'clock."

"Twelve thirty." Sasha's earlier time overrode her mother's. "I don't want him late because he forgot what time it was. You be here at twelve-thirty, Matt. Okay?"

He grinned and mock-saluted her with three fingers. "You're the boss."

The breakfast continued with laughter and loud talking. Alanah ate her breakfast quietly. It smelled wonderful, but she couldn't bring herself to eat much. A sadness ate into her appetite. She was uber-aware of Caleb, and he smiled at her several times. Just like at the rehearsal dinner. They kept staring at each other. There was nothing for it but to try and enjoy the day and be the best support to Sasha she could be. Descending into sadness was not going to help and would spoil Sasha's day.

Finally, Caleb left with Matt. Mia and Lucy helped their mother clear up the breakfast, and Alanah went with Sasha to prepare for the hairdresser.

"You and Caleb are a sad pair," Sasha said as she lined up the seat in front of the bedroom mirror.

"I'm not going to argue with you."

"It breaks my heart to see my twin brother and my best friend so sad. Can't you do something to make it work?"

"What? What solution would you suggest?"

Sasha bit her lip. Had Alanah been too harsh?

"Don't worry about us, Sash. This is your day of joy, and I know Caleb would want you to enjoy it as much as I do."

Sasha took Alanah's hand and gave it a squeeze. "It's been so great having you here the last few months. I'm going to miss you when you go home."

"I hope Australia will be one of your destinations when you and Derek are planning travel next."

"That will take longer to save for, but I would like to go back again one day. Show Derek where I spent my high school years."

"Don't leave it too long, Sash."

Sasha gave Alanah a warm hug. Alanah couldn't help the tears that stung her eyes. That was the trouble with long-distance relationships. There would always be a parting, and video chat aside, it was still hard.

CHAPTER EIGHTEEN

Caleb's job was to assist Derek with anything he wanted on his wedding day. Derek's best mate had most of it in hand, and good job too. The burden of knowing Alanah was leaving in two days was weighing on Caleb. His heart was heavy, and he was not the man to rely on today. Alanah couldn't stay. He knew that. He'd always known that. But letting her leave was tearing him up.

"You need to cheer up, mate." Alex was at the church when the men arrived ready for the wedding.

Caleb gave a forced smile.

"Sasha and Derek won't thank you when they get their wedding photos back with you looking like your dog just died."

"You're right."

Alex was helping with the music for the wedding. Caleb was glad he was there. The last few weeks had been difficult, especially with Kyla still airing her warped view of what had happened. He hoped that once Alanah went back to Australia, Kyla would stop with her incessant insinuations. They hadn't just been uncomfortable for him. They had caused people who were usually open and friendly to be cautious, even difficult.

Pastor Dean Wilder was officiating the wedding. Things had been strained between Caleb and him ever since he'd asked Caleb to stand down from worship and youth. There was no point at which the pastor had believed Caleb—that Kyla had lied or even exaggerated. Caleb had been maligned. The thing that boggled his mind the most was that apparently, Kyla still hoped he would come back to her. Fat chance.

Caleb helped set the table with the official paperwork, helped Alex run a couple of cables, allowed Derek's mother to pin a buttonhole flower on his suit lapel, then he waited.

The church began to fill with guests. Caleb smiled at the Kennedy aunts, uncles, and cousins, and Gran and Gramps as they arrived and took a seat.

"Don't you look handsome?" Gran was her usual self, full of compliments as Caleb approached to greet them. These two precious people were the reason Mom and Dad had decided to return to Trinity Lakes. It had been the right decision, but so much pain for him as well. He smiled at Gran as she took her seat on the front row on the Kennedy side of the church. She blew him a kiss.

Another twenty minutes and the seats were full. Pastor Dean walked up the aisle from the door, took his position at the front and addressed the congregation.

"Ladies and gentlemen, the bride has arrived. Would you please stand?"

Why on earth was his heart thumping with eager anticipation? He loved his twin sister. No doubt about that, but what was with the racing pulse?

The bridesmaids entered first, Mia followed by Lucy, then his heart stopped. Alanah was gorgeous. She'd been gorgeous this morning, all freshly washed and messy hair, but this was another level of gorgeous. He struggled to swallow the lump in his throat as his mouth had gone completely dry. Then she peered up at him. Oh, Lord. Why was this so difficult? He'd lost perspective, unable to hear the music, and the people in the church had faded to insignificance.

It wasn't until Sasha entered the church and began her bridal procession that Caleb was able to get his thoughts into order. Sasha. The person who'd been with him his whole life, shared every experience, who was about to be married to another person. Sasha was his pride in that moment. Derek had better treat her well, or there'd be trouble. It didn't take more than two minutes to realize Derek was as in love with Sasha as Caleb was with Alanah. More, given he was prepared to commit to her for life.

The ceremony was beautiful. Mom cried. Gran cried. He wanted to cry but didn't.

Once the party was outside the church, people milling around congratulating the bride and groom, Gran came up and took Caleb's arm.

"Why on earth don't you marry that girl, Caleb? It's so obvious."

"What girl?" As if he didn't know.

"Your friend from Australia."

"I can't ask her to leave her home and family. She is really close to them. Leaving would make her miserable."

"Who said anything about her leaving home and family?"

"Usually when you get married, you have to live in the same place."

"Of course."

Caleb raised his eyebrows at his gran in question.

"Why don't you go and live there? You've been there before?"

The thought hit him like a freight train. "I can't leave here."

"Why not?"

"Because of …" Because of what? He searched his mind for all the reasons he was sure must be there.

"The world is a small place, Caleb. I let your mother go

touring the world when she was younger. That was where she met your dad, and then they continued to roam the planet."

"But they came back here for you, eventually."

"I'm glad they came back, but traveling and experiencing the world was in their blood."

Caleb reviewed the places he'd lived as a child. Before their years in Australia, they'd spent a couple of years in New Zealand, and before that, Hawaii. His sense of place wasn't as strong as Alanah's. But his family connection was just as strong. Just watching his twin kissing and laughing with her new husband brought a strange feeling. Was it loss? Sasha wouldn't always be there for him from now on. She was her own woman, and now a life partner with her husband.

"Caleb. Pay attention. We need to get some shots of the bridal party." Sasha waved him over, then began to boss everyone around. The photographer had the patience of a saint. By the time they had been manipulated and shuffled according to size, Caleb found he was standing directly behind Alanah, inches between them.

"Smile." The photographer had been all but turning somersaults in an attempt to get the best expressions from his subjects. Derek put his hands at Sasha's waist. How Caleb wished he had the courage to do the same with Alanah. But he didn't.

When they were released from posing, Alanah turned and smiled up at him. "How do you feel seeing her get married?"

"I didn't realize how hard it would be." Time for truth.

"I know, right?"

"It's going to be hard saying goodbye to you as well."

"Caleb, don't. Please." She wore the same sad expression that reflected how he felt.

"I wish there was something—"

"But there isn't. It's awful now, but I'll leave and we'll both get over it. You'll meet someone and be happy."

"I doubt it."

"We're just caught in the emotion of it right now. Best we accept the inevitable."

Caleb studied her face. She was right. "Could we just enjoy the day today?"

"That's the plan."

"Will you dance with me at the reception?"

She gave him a weak smile and nodded. "How can I refuse?"

The crowd outside the church surged as Sasha and Derek got into the ribbon-bedecked car. He had to focus on today and what it meant for Sasha. He would dance with Alanah tonight, then they would say goodbye, and that would be the end of it.

If only his heart would cooperate.

———

IT HAD BEEN A MAMMOTH EFFORT, but Alanah had determined to throw off her melancholy for the sake of Sasha and Derek. The reception had been fun, sitting next to Sasha, who was always the life of the party. Today, she was amped up with the joy of becoming Derek's wife. Thankfully, her joy managed to eclipse the looming separation. Caleb was seated several seats away on the other side almost out of sight.

Then came the first dance for the bride and groom. Sasha was beautiful. She and Derek didn't just look good together, they were made for each other. He was such a kind person, and his amiable personality was a perfect balance to Sasha's intensity.

"Would the bridal party please join Sasha and Derek on the dance floor?"

"Do you want to swap with me?" Lucy whispered to Alanah.

"Do you mind?" Alanah whispered back as she stood up from the table.

Lucy had been partnered with Caleb all day, and the thought

of dancing with Caleb was much more appealing than dancing with Derek's best man, who was married and who she hardly knew.

"You've only got tomorrow before you leave. Make the most of the time you have."

Was it wise to be engaging in this close physical activity with Caleb given her imminent goodbye? Wise or not, Lucy had gone to the best man and was obviously explaining the change of partner to him. Caleb only appeared confused for a second, then he came across and held out his hand.

Wise or not, Alanah was not going to refuse.

"It's been a beautiful day." Alanah easily fell into rhythm with the love ballad the band was playing. It was natural being held together in this dance.

"I am so proud of her, Alanah. I had somehow dreaded seeing her get married, but today has settled all my worries."

"You'll miss her?"

"We both went to different colleges, so we've been apart before."

"Except college was only a temporary experience. This is forever."

"I know. But we've grown up now. It was bound to happen. I'm just glad she married Derek. He's a top bloke."

Alanah smiled. They fell into silence as they continued to dance. Caleb tugged her a little closer and she couldn't resist. This wasn't the stiff awkward dance she'd had with the unrelated bridal attendants. The energy that hummed between them was real. He must feel it as much as she did.

"So you'll get back just in time for the new school year?"

"Caleb Kennedy. You know that September is the beginning of our final term before summer. You haven't been gone that long."

He grinned. "I forgot for a second. I plot everything by the calendar I run here."

"I considered staying until Thanksgiving, considering we don't celebrate it, and it would have been a great cultural experience."

Caleb's face lit up with a hopeful expression.

"I can't though. I've taken four months off, and I don't want to push."

"Have you been here all this time without pay?"

"There has been some holiday pay, some long-service leave pay and the rest leave without pay. I need to get back or they might not be so friendly about holding my job."

"So you're working admin at the local council?"

She nodded.

"Not interested in using your social work degree?" Caleb stepped out and lifted their joined hands, and Alanah did a neat little spin that landed her back in the warmth of his embrace.

"I might see if there's an organization that sends social workers to the remote rural districts."

"I remember Booleroo Whim as a stable community, but surely there would be some need for social work." Another spin. It was fun, especially the landing.

"It's getting more and more likely, what with persistent drought, associated family breakdown and stress, and more people coming out from the city because of cheap housing. They often come with some sort of personal crisis. I think it's worth investigating."

"What about the church there?"

"Pastors are getting more and more reluctant to do counseling because Australia seems to have caught onto the idea of litigation. There are a whole stack of compliance and duty of care ramifications that now affect pastors and others working with people."

"Who is the pastor at the Booleroo Whim church now?"

"Pastor Walter has finally retired, and they don't currently have anyone to take his place. The congregation is too small and rural communities are often overlooked."

"That's sad. How do you fellowship?"

"We still hold church services, but it's run by the three elders."

"All volunteer farmers, no doubt."

"Pretty much. Dad is one of them, and I pitch in occasionally."

"You'd be good at that."

Alanah smiled.

The song finished, they joined with the crowd in light applause. Alanah reluctantly stepped back from Caleb.

"Now it's time for the father-daughter dance."

Caleb took Alanah's hand, and they left the dance floor together as James came to dance with Sasha and Derek's mother came to dance with him. Alanah expected Caleb would leave and go back to his seat, but he didn't. They stood at the edge of the dance floor, and he continued to hold her hand. It felt right, even though it was probably wrong.

"Do you want to step outside for a breath of fresh air?" Caleb whispered in her ear.

She didn't bother to answer but followed as he led the way outside. This wasn't about fresh air, and she knew it.

"I wanted to say goodbye properly to you." Caleb still held her hand, and then turned to put his arms fully around her.

"What about tomorrow?" *Please don't let this be the end. Please.*

"I can't, Alanah. I need to say goodbye tonight and leave it. Drawing it out is killing me."

It was killing her as well, but she didn't want to argue. She just snuggled closer into his embrace, laying her head on his shoulder. Why couldn't she stay here forever? Would he ask her to stay? Could she stay if he asked her? It was all too hard.

"Alanah?"

She could hear passion in his tone. Lifting her head from his shoulder, she studied his expression—eyes liquid and intense, his Adam's apple moving as he swallowed.

"I love you. I always have."

Caleb touched the side of her face with his warm hand and for a split second, she leaned into this gentle touch.

These were words she wanted to hear, but they angered her at the same time. This was stupid. What use was it to be in love with someone when there was no way they could be together?

"I can't, Caleb. I'm sorry." She pulled away from him and fled back inside. She avoided the bridal table and went straight to the bathroom. There were a couple of women touching up their makeup at the mirror. She didn't know them, thank goodness. Finding an empty stall, she went in, latched the door, sat down on the closed toilet seat, and wept.

CHAPTER NINETEEN

Alanah's brain was full of fudge. The last forty-eight hours had been awful. Saying goodbye to Sasha should have been full of joy, but they both knew that when Sasha returned from her honeymoon Alanah would be gone. Hugs and tears and more hugs. Then she'd said goodbye to the family, minus Caleb. Lucy had driven her to Spokane, with more tears and hugs. The passenger who sat next to her on the first flight to LA must have thought someone had died—or that her heart was broken. It was.

The rest of the trip home was long and tiring. She lost a day crossing the international date line and arrived at Adelaide International Airport bedraggled and bereft. Her sister, Kelly, was there to meet her, having brought her kids down to the city to visit the dentist. Thankfully she seemed to accept Alanah's disconnected state as a result of jet lag.

When they arrived back at the farm at Booleroo Whim, she had a cup of tea and a toasted sandwich, then retreated to her bedroom. She was exhausted from the travel, despite having slept a good two hours during the car ride from the city. She was thankful for the excuse to hide from her parents and Mitch.

What was with Mitch, anyway? Kelly had said he had a girl-friend, and apparently, she was boarding with them. Mum and Dad had returned home from their caravan trip around Australia, and Mitch—the brother she thought would probably die single—had a girlfriend. She threw herself on the bed and buried her head in the pillow. Her body clock and her emotional clock were both still set to Trinity Lakes time. It was just on four in the afternoon, but a quick calculation told her it was 9:30 p.m. yesterday back in Washington State. Her heart tugged. Caleb would have come back from staying at his mate's place. The Kennedys would be sitting around the lounge, talking about their first week back at school after summer break. She missed them. But could she give up her life here?

It was strange how connected she was to this farm and her family. The Australian government now recognized how strong the connection to country was for the first Australians, and the more Alanah heard about it, the more she identified. She knew how she would feel if she was forced to abandon the land on which she had grown up, as the Aboriginal people had been forced to. She had a strong sense of place, too strong to ignore.

Why couldn't she have fallen in love with one of the other boys she went to school with? One of the boys who went to take over their family farm? Someone like Mitch. Eww. Her brother. That was the wrong image. But then, as she went through the other young farmers she'd been to school with, they got the same reaction as thinking of Mitch. Eww. There was only one boy from school she could be interested in, and he was an American who lived in Trinity Lakes, on the other side of the world. It was hopeless.

Alanah pulled the cover around her to ward off the chill of early spring. She was going to sleep according to the advice she'd heard in a sermon recently. When you can't control the situation, and you are overwhelmed, do what Jesus did in the middle of the storm. Sleep. Rest in the rock of all ages, and leave the situation with Him.

———

THANKSGIVING WAS BECOMING Caleb's favorite time of year. When he'd been traveling the world with his parents, they'd acknowledged Thanksgiving, but it wasn't such a big deal in countries that weren't connected to the American holiday. But the years since they'd returned to Trinity Lakes, Mom had pulled out all the stops. She had tried in years previous as well, but now they were home, Thanksgiving was the focus of the whole community.

Caleb had stayed at Jason's until Sasha had returned from the Caribbean, then he'd returned home. But he had made a decision to start searching for a place of his own. It was time. Of course, he would need to increase his income, as cost of living was going to increase dramatically without Mom and Dad as the fail-safe support.

"You're still here." Gran kissed Caleb on the cheek as she came in from the snow outside. She shrugged off her faux fur coat and handed it to him.

"Where did you think I'd be?"

"Australia."

"Australia?" His heart gave a thump. He knew what she meant but played dumb anyway.

"Don't be silly, Caleb. I must say I am surprised to see you here."

She was determined, and he knew exactly what she was referring to. But would he go there? It had been over two months and he had told himself he would get over Alanah. That was the official line, but if he were honest—if Gran pushed him —he would break down and admit he missed her like a man gasping for air. Should he allow Gran the opportunity?

"I'm trying to forget her, Gran."

"Why?"

"Because—"

"If you tell me that she lives too far away, so help me—"

"So help you? Help you how? You seem to have it all worked out."

"Nothing could be simpler."

"You think I should pack up my life here and move back Down Under?"

"If that's what it takes."

"But what about Mom and Dad? You and Gramps? My job and friends here?"

"Your job. You're working in a music store, and you having earned a bachelor in Christian ministry. Is that what you plan to do the rest of your life?"

She had a point. He'd already started to think about getting another job—one that would support an independent lifestyle—independent from his parents.

"I'd miss home."

"Really? How attached are you to Trinity Lakes?"

"This is where family is."

"Gramps and I won't be here much longer."

"What? Where are you going?"

The aged woman lifted her gaze toward heaven and pointed.

"Gran. You shouldn't talk like that."

"We're not here forever, Caleb, and you can't hang around here for our sake, or your parents. If you know where your heart is, go there and start a new life."

"You make it sound easy."

"Talk to your parents. They know what it's about. They won't stop you."

She reached up and patted his cheek. "But for goodness' sake, make a decision and get moving. I can't bear to see you moping around like this."

She moved into the family room, leaving him stunned. The rest of the family were busy getting the food and the table ready for their Thanksgiving meal. Moping around? He wasn't moping—was he? He loved every person in this house. His parents, brother, three sisters, and his new brother-in-law, Derek. And Gran and Gramps, of course. How hard would it be to leave them all behind and go pursue life on the other side of the world?

By the time Mom had everyone rallied around the large dining table, Caleb's thoughts had been around the world and back. There were possibilities that needed further investigation, problems to address, but nothing insurmountable. Mom and Dad had done this before. They would help him if he asked.

"What about you, Caleb?"

He was jolted from his thoughts and realized that they had begun the traditional round the table giving of thanks.

"Ah sorry. My turn?"

"Tick-tock. The turkey isn't getting any younger." Matt tapped his watch.

"I'm thankful for Gran and her wisdom."

Gran leaned back in her chair and clapped her hands in triumph, a huge smile decorating her face. "Praise the Lord," she said with full gusto.

"What's that about?" Dad asked. A quick scan around the table revealed that almost everyone was puzzled by Gran's spontaneous eruption of joy.

"I'll let him tell you," Gran said, smiling and jerking her thumb in Caleb's direction.

All eyes turned on him. Talk about being put on the spot. Should he pretend he didn't understand?

"Go on, Caleb. Tell them." Apparently, Gran was not going to let him hide.

"I think I'm going to investigate moving to Australia again."

"You're going to marry Alanah?" Sasha. Very like her grandmother in her enthusiasm about matchmaking, and in leaping ten steps ahead.

"Easy, turbo. I'm just thinking about the logistics of living away from you lot."

"If you move back there and marry Alanah, we'll have somewhere to stay when we come to visit. It's a great plan." Lucy seemed to be as bad as Sasha, but how did Mom and Dad take his announcement? He glanced in their direction.

"I'm thankful for Gran's wisdom too," Mom said. "And though we'll miss you, I'm glad you're going to pursue the love of your life."

Dad nodded in agreement. Had they been talking about this behind his back? From the knowing smiles, it seemed entirely possible.

———

CHRISTMAS WAS the best time of the year. At least, it used to be, but this warm Christmas Eve, Alanah was feeling blue. Three months she'd been home, carefully directing her thoughts away from Caleb and all that had eventuated during her visit to North America. She'd gone back to her admin job and engaged in all her usual community activities. Anything to keep her mind from going back to Trinity Lakes. It seemed to be worse than the first time they'd been ripped apart. They'd been kids then, and Mum had encouraged her she'd get over her first love when she met the right man.

But her first love was the right man. At least, that was what her heart told her, and she was having a terrible time telling her heart otherwise.

She tried not to be jealous when she saw Mitch and his new girlfriend, Charlie, preparing for their first Christmas together. It was sweet and sickening all at the same time. Her rugged, scruffy brother had changed since Charlie had literally blown into his life. They would probably announce their engagement this Christmas. That would seem the most likely thing. And she would smile and pretend to be overjoyed, when all the while, her heart would be sitting in the corner and crying, lonely for Caleb.

"Are you ready?" Mum popped her head in Alanah's bedroom door.

"More to the point, are Dad and Mitch ready?" Alanah had been helping them with reaping earlier in the day, but she had left them to it in the late afternoon, wanting to help her mother get things ready for the carol's night. It was the middle of harvest and getting farmers in from their headers and cleaned up was an experience in nagging.

"Mitch wanted to stay out for another couple of hours." Mum was packing some Christmas baking into her Tupperware.

"He'll miss the service."

"He'll probably get there in the nick of time."

"Covered in dust and chaff? Is Charlie coming?"

"She's driving back from Adelaide and will probably arrive at the same time as Mitch."

"So is Dad driving into town with us?"

Mum picked up the basket of baking. "He's just combing his hair now, but—"

"But? We're going to be late."

"We won't be late, Lani. We're two hours early."

"Because we're part of the organizing committee. And Dad—"

"Dad has another errand to run. It's going to be fine. When did you become so angsty?"

Angsty? She wasn't angsty. She prided herself on being cool and calm under pressure. And they weren't even under pressure. Mum was right. They still had a couple of hours before the church service. Then there was another hour between the

THE OCEAN BETWEEN US

service and the outdoor carol singing. She took a deep breath. She was overcompensating, trying to hide her sadness.

She picked up a second basket and followed Mum outside to the car. It was going to be a cracker of a night for outdoor carol singing. The sun was still warm even as it sat lower in the sky, not a breath of wind. She glanced at her mobile phone to see the temperature. A balmy twenty-eight degrees. What was that in Fahrenheit? Why was she always trying to calculate what the temperature might be in Trinity Lakes? No. She was not going to be forever dwelling on Trinity Lakes and the people there. All right. On Caleb, who lived there.

"The weather's going to be great for our outdoor carols." Mum got into the driver's seat and started the engine.

Alanah wanted to face palm. She'd just talked herself out of opening the converter on the weather app, but it drew her. The curiosity was killing her. A quick search and she found the temperature converter. Twenty-eight degrees Celsius was Eighty-two degrees Fahrenheit. What was the weather in Trinity Lakes? Thirty-seven degrees. She converted. She had to, because thirty-seven degrees Celsius would have them all melting. Only three degrees Celsius, just above freezing. It was the middle of winter there, and short days. No doubt they would be rugged up inside by the fire, drinking some warm Christmas drink that was unfamiliar to her.

"Whatcha doing?" Mum cast a glance in her direction.

"Obsessing."

"Over what? The weather?"

Alanah nodded. She was sprung.

"Typical farmer's daughter. It's perfect reaping weather."

Great. She had a diversion from her real activity. She wasn't prepared to admit to anyone in her family that her heart was still attached to a place on the other side of the planet.

"You don't seem to be your normal cheery self," Mum said as they approached the outer limit of Booleroo Whim.

"What makes you say that?"

"You're angsty, for one thing."

Alanah opened her mouth to protest, but her mother cut her off.

"Christmas is usually your favorite time of year. You've seemed distracted since returning from overseas."

Alanah nodded. She wasn't going to deny it.

"You had a great time, didn't you?"

Alanah nodded again. She'd shown them all the photos and videos she'd taken. She'd talked about her adventure in Canada. She'd told them all about the Kennedy family and passed along their good wishes. She had been full of enthusiasm at the time, but as the weeks had worn on, she had to admit she was pining.

Mum pulled the car up in front of the church. "Whatever is on your mind, Lani, it will work out all right. Don't miss out on the joy of Christmas by letting it get you down." Mum patted her knee. "Come on. Let's get this stuff into the church kitchen and set out ready for later."

———

WHAT A CONTRAST. Four days ago, Caleb was in his puffer jacket, beanie, and scarf, saying goodbye to teary relatives and stoic friends. Today he was standing on a farmhouse veranda in shorts and t-shirt, taking in the landscape of his youth. So many memories flooded to the surface. Summer harvest time. The golden paddocks heavy with wheat and barley. Combine harvesters—headers—could be seen in just about every direction he looked, dust and chaff blowing out behind as the precious grain was being brought in. He'd helped Mitch Walker and other mates from high school with harvesting a few times. It was hot work, and one wouldn't want to suffer from asthma or hay fever. This industrious scene sat with the magnificent Mount Remarkable as a backdrop. So different from the Amer-

THE OCEAN BETWEEN US

ican Rockies. Mount Remarkable was part of the world-famous Flinders Ranges, magnificent rock and land structures that stood up on the open plains. Covered in the various gum, wattle and acacia, the mountain always appeared blue, but rarely had snow. The climate was too hot and dry for that.

He breathed in again. A summer shower had passed through about an hour ago. It hadn't amounted to much—didn't even settle the dust—but the smell. He remembered the smell of summer rain on dry stubble from his youth. It was a smell that should be bottled.

Caleb's cell pinged. It was the message service that ran from the internet. He'd logged into Pastor Walter's home internet when he'd arrived so he could keep in contact with everyone back home. He flipped the phone open. Kyla. Really? It must be close to midnight in Trinity Lakes. What could she want?

I just heard you'd left the country. I would have thought you might have said good-bye.

Did he really want to do this now? Things between him and Kyla had ended badly and had only gotten worse. It was his fault. Right from the start, it had been his fault. He should have resisted getting involved with her in the first place. The relationship had been convenient—that was all—and he'd allowed her and everybody else's opinion to cajole him into making it more. He knew she wasn't the one but had allowed her to believe she was. It was his fault. He got up and went inside the house.

"All good, Caleb?" Pastor Walter asked as he came into the kitchen.

"Just have to answer a message."

"Someone from home?" The older pastor seemed interested.

"I have a situation there I haven't completely resolved. I should have before I left to come out here."

"The church elders here are keen to have you take on our congregation, Caleb, but we need to know your heart is in it, and that you can settle here. It would be hard on the people to connect with you, only to have you decide in six months that you need to go back to your folks."

Caleb nodded.

Pastor Walter raised his bushy eyebrows in a question.

"You're right. I think it might be time I had a difficult conversation."

"The decision is likely to be a huge personal sacrifice for you. We need to know you're sure."

"I'll be thinking and praying about it over the Christmas break."

Pastor Walter nodded in obvious approval.

"Is it okay if I make a video call? I need to settle this situation."

"The church service is in an hour. I hope you'll be able to come. It would be good for you to see how it is, given the decision you're about to make."

"I hope it won't take that long, but I really need to sort this out."

"Today's technology is amazing."

Caleb nodded. That was the upside. When they'd lived here before, they'd only had expensive phone calls to keep in touch with the grandparents.

Pastor Walter got up from his chair. "I'll give you some space."

Caleb leaned back in the kitchen chair. It was time. If he was going to commit to this role, he couldn't leave the situation with Kyla as it was. He hoped she was still awake.

"Caleb." Kyla's voice came before she connected the video, the same smiling image from a few years ago. Her hair tied up in a ponytail, and a complete summer look.

"Hey, Kyla. Turn your video on."

It took a moment to get the proper video connection.

"I'm glad you called." She was smiling live but wrapped up in her woolly winter dressing gown.

"Hope it's not too late for you."

"Not at all. I couldn't think of anything I'd like better."

Right. She was going to push this still.

"Kyla, I need to apologize—"

"You don't have to, Caleb. I forgive—"

"No. Wait. Let me finish what I need to say."

"I forgive you anyway." She gave a smile.

"I'm not sure you understand how things are."

"I know you need some space, and a trip Down Under sounds like fun. I can't wait to come with you next time."

"There won't be a next time. I'm planning to move down here for good."

There was silence, and the expression on Kyla's face was ... was something. He couldn't quite figure out what.

"When I said our relationship was over, I meant it, Kyla. I'm not coming back." He saw her take a breath ready to launch, but he cut her off. "It's my fault. And I want to apologize."

She aborted the launch and closed her mouth.

"I let you talk me into getting engaged when I never felt it was right."

"What do you mean?"

"Right from the word go. We hung out together, and that was okay as co-youth leaders, but I should not have allowed you to think we could date, let alone get married."

She opened her mouth again.

"It's my fault, Kyla. And I'm prepared to wear the blame. I should have been more decisive about what I believed was right."

"And Alanah?"

"She has nothing to do with it."

"But you've gone down there to see her."

"Maybe. I'm not sure that will work out either, yet, but if it does or if it doesn't, you and I are not going to happen. I was wrong to ever let you think it could."

She was stunned. Her expression had shades of different emotions going across. One moment shock, the next anger, the next despair, then anger again, then a pleading look. It was hard to watch, but he was the one who had brought her to this place. He had to watch, and he had to take responsibility.

"I'm sorry, Kyla."

Tears welled in her eyes, then her face hardened. He braced himself for the fallout.

"How could you do this just before Christmas? How could you, Caleb?"

He shook his head. Before he'd left, Jason had said to him that Kyla sounded like she struggled with narcissistic personality disorder. He'd searched the condition online and the characteristics fit to some degree, perhaps but she wasn't typical in every sense. Whatever. She had proven time and again that she was emotionally dysfunctional, having to control every situation according to how she felt.

"I'm sorry, Kyla. You can tell everyone it's my fault. I will wear it."

"You're too much of a coward to face your responsibility here, so you've run away to Australia."

She was back to using the cutting words. He sighed. He'd done what he could to repair that which was his fault. It seemed like it wasn't going to happen.

"I don't ever want to see you again."

The connection cut abruptly. "Merry Christmas, Kyla," he said to the blank screen.

He took a deep breath. Was his coming back to Booleroo Whim too soon? It had been five months since he'd broken it off with Kyla, and yet she had persisted in pretending it was just a short break, a bump in the road. He hoped she fully understood now, because he wanted that chapter of his life to be closed and not to open again.

The call hadn't taken as long as he'd thought it might. Pastor Walter and his wife were putting some things together ready to take for the outdoor caroling after the church service. His mind raced back twelve years, the last time he'd been to an Australian Christmas event—late sunset, warm evening, skies full of brilliant stars. That night he'd kissed Alanah with full intention of formalizing their fledgling relationship. But within a week, he'd had to break it off completely.

He dug through his suitcase for a pair of better-than-average cargo shorts. He was glad Mom had advised him what to pack as he'd forgotten just how dramatic the temperature difference would be, flying out of winter straight into summer.

"You ready to go?" Pastor Walter had his Bible and notebook ready to deliver the Christmas Eve sermon.

"I'm ready. Is this too casual?" Caleb indicated his shorts, t-shirt, and good walking boots.

"Given some of the men will come in from the tractor without changing, I think you'll pass."

There was no doubt Aussie churchgoing attire was way more casual than what he'd been used to. He was almost tempted to wear flip-flops—the footwear that caused so many laughs. His high school mates had called them thongs, as did every other Aussie, but he couldn't quite bring himself to say the word. His American sensibilities wouldn't allow it.

"Did you get some closure on that other matter?" the older man asked.

"Yes and no. I've done my best. There isn't anything else I can do to make it right, I'm afraid."

"Well, set your heart towards the Lord. There are some things in life that can't be resolved, no matter how hard we try. Some things we just have to leave with Him."

Caleb nodded as he got in the back seat of the car. Pastor Walter had been part-time pastor, part-time farmer. The churches out in these remote communities were never big enough to support a full-time wage, so Pastor Walter had lived on his family farm and done church work one or two days a week. He'd stepped back from it now, hence the opportunity for Caleb to be considered.

"Have you spoken to the high school principal yet?" June Walter asked as her husband pulled the car out of the farmyard.

"I have." He hadn't met the man before, but apparently Caleb's parents' reputation still lingered at the district high school.

"What was his response?" Pastor Walter asked.

"He was keen but couldn't make any firm promises until they get the new school year up and running in late January."

"From what I know, there's only one piano teacher in the district, and she's past retirement age. Having a music teacher who is young and can connect with the young people would be a huge blessing," Mrs. Walter said.

Caleb smiled. Mrs. Walter was encouraging. He wondered how many young people from this farming community would have an interest in music. The principal was enthusiastic about the possibilities. If he could get three days' worth of work teaching music, it was likely the church could support him for the other two—if he decided it was right to stay.

They travelled down the dusty drive to the main road, still dusty, and further until they came to the bitumen sealed road that led into town. Caleb's heart thumped harder than usual.

Alanah would be at the service.

She didn't know he was here. She didn't know he was even coming, unless Sasha had let the cat out of the bag. He hoped not. He'd wanted to see if there was something here for him first, before letting Alanah know.

CHAPTER TWENTY

Alanah's grandmother had been the church pianist for as long as she could remember. Grandma still played on occasion, simply because there weren't many musicians who could fill the role. But Grandma knew how to play, especially when it came to hymns and carols. These traditional songs evoked all the wonderful memories of childhood. As the small congregation began to sing, Alanah let the words and joyous Christmas spirit bring peace to her soul. This celebration of Christ's coming was the high point in the year.

Pastor Walter had agreed to deliver the Christmas sermon, despite being retired. Sometimes the old and familiar was a comfort.

"We're going to try something new this year," Pastor Walter said. "I saw it on one of those Hallmark movies that June loves to watch."

Alanah smiled. She loved to watch the sweet Hallmark Christmas movies too. It reminded her of … stop. She would not go there.

"June is going to hand out candles to everyone. When I've lit mine at the front, I'll pass the flame to the first person on the front row, who'll pass it along the rows, until all our candles are lit."

It was eight o'clock and the sun was not quite down yet. Still. "And be careful. We are in the middle of fire danger season. If we mess it up this year, we won't do it again."

Everyone laughed.

As the flame was passed along the rows, Grandma played Silent Night.

"Do we all have a lit candle?"

Alanah smiled. The congregation wasn't that big. It hadn't taken long.

"Before we sing our final hymn, I'd like everyone to take a few moments to go to someone and swap candles, as a symbol of sharing the light and love of Christ with each other."

This was so Hallmark, minus the freezing, dark conditions, and if you could ignore the sundresses and board shorts being worn in church.

Alanah turned to see who she'd like to exchange her candle with and froze. Caleb was standing at the end of her row, his focus directly on her. Caleb.

"How … what…?" She only mouthed the words. There was a solemn exchange of light going on. It wasn't the time for loud outbursts.

"Excuse me. Pardon me." Caleb edged past Mum and Dad. They didn't appear surprised. A question popped into Alanah's mind but was quickly squashed. What did it matter? He was here, holding out his candle to her. Who cares how he got here?

"May I share the light of Christ with you?" he asked.

"May I share my life with you?" Did she just say that? Her eyes rushed to meet his. He wore a grin to allay the look of horror that must be evident on her face.

He leaned closer and whispered in her ear. "That will be the first item on the agenda when we get to talk later."

Her face broke into a matching grin. She noticed her parents closely observing the exchange, and threw them a frown. "Did you know?" she mouthed the words to them. They just smiled inanely back.

"May I stand with you for the final hymn?" Caleb asked.

She swapped the candle to her left hand and threaded her hand with his.

"Try going anywhere else," she said.

———

Nobody seemed particularly surprised. Mum and Dad greeted Caleb after the service as if it were perfectly normal for him to be there. The other two elders in the church shook his hand and welcomed him but didn't make any of the inane statements she'd expect. No "fancy seeing you here" or "it's been ages".

Pastor and Mrs. Walter asked him if he needed a ride to the park where the carols were being held, an offer he rejected. Everyone seemed to know. Everyone except Mitch.

"Mate. Fancy seeing you here. Long time no see." Mitch grabbed Caleb's hand in a brother-like clasp and did that bump-shoulder kind of hug. "What brings you back here to Booleroo Whim?"

Mitch would probably figure it out if he took two seconds to see that Caleb still held Alanah's hand, but brothers were never particularly quick on the uptake. But that might have been jumping ahead of herself. Caleb held her hand, and she hoped she knew what brought him back. She stopped and listened with anticipation to what Caleb would say.

"I heard you needed a pastor here in Booleroo Whim."

A pastor? Alanah turned a slight frown in Caleb's direction.

"And I heard music tutors were a bit thin on the ground out here."

199

"Really?" Mitch. Honestly, he could be incredibly thick sometimes.

"Is there a good livelihood in all that?" Alanah asked, knowing full well it was a terrible livelihood. He could do so much better in a more populated place.

Caleb squeezed her hand. "Catch you later, Mitch." He moved towards the door of the church.

"If you're going to the carols, I'd like to introduce you to my fiancée," Mitch called after them.

Alanah did a double take. Fiancée? He'd finally proposed to Charlie? But who could be interested in her brother's love life when there was one of her own to pay attention to? It wasn't too hard to gain the exit and walk out into the small parking area.

"Did you come with your parents?" Caleb asked.

Alanah nodded. "From Pastor Walter's question before, I assume you're staying with them?"

"Yes, ma'am."

"So we're without wheels?"

"But not without legs. A walk on this beautiful warm evening is just what I was hoping for."

Alanah smiled and allowed herself to move so close to Caleb that he put his arm around her waist.

"I'm so glad to see you, Caleb."

"I'm glad to be here."

"So, a pastor and music tutor, hm?"

"That's the plan at this stage, but that depends on one thing before I fully commit to it."

Alanah felt a warm surge from her stomach to her chest. It seemed obvious. She wouldn't play coy. "What's the missing piece?"

They were approaching the park where locals were gathering with picnic blankets and fake candles, but Caleb pulled her to a stop. He turned her to face him.

"You're the missing piece, Alanah, and you know it."

She smiled. She knew, but she wanted to hear it spelled out.

"Will you marry me?" Caleb's face was serious. He had doubts?

"I guess the intercontinental thing has to be discussed, doesn't it?"

"My folks and I have had a long discussion. I love them but being with them isn't as important as being with you."

"It's a big sacrifice to make, Caleb. I know. I've thought about it and found I couldn't do it. I'm sorry. I feel like I've let you down."

"The sacrifice aspect is what has kept us apart for so many years. I get it, and I've thought about it. I believe I can make my life here just as well as in Trinity Lakes."

"Really?" There was no keeping the excitement out of her voice.

"It's not so hard, really. We travelled so much as kids— Hawaii, New Zealand, then here. But the best years of my life were here. I might sound American, but just being here has made me feel Aussie again. I know I'll fit. And I know I have a love for the community, enough to be a pastor and community leader. All I need is a partner—a wife—who loves the community and people as much as I do and who can help me. Someone with training in social work would be perfect."

"I know someone." Alanah grinned and threw her arms around his neck. "Pick me."

Caleb grinned back and rested his forehead against hers. "That's a yes, then?"

"That's a heck yes."

Caleb stifled a laugh as he dove in for a kiss. Then the laughter mellowed, and the kiss grew deep and lingering.

"Something I should know?" Mitch's voice broke the spell and they pulled back.

Alanah smiled at her brother.

"I was going to introduce you to Charlie, my fiancée," Mitch said, pointing to the smiling young woman who stood next to him.

"I was going to introduce you to my fiancée as well," Caleb replied.

Alanah didn't care about any of it. She'd just shot to the moon and back and was still trying to find her feet. Christmas Eve had dawned with a longing sadness. Now she was about to join her community in singing time-honored Christmas carols and waving fake candles while standing with Caleb, her fiancé. The joy and contentment enveloping her was something she would remember for many Christmases to come.

BEFORE YOU GO:

If you enjoyed this story, would you mind taking a few minutes to pop a review on the site where you purchased *The Ocean Between Us*, or on the Good Reads website. Every review helps me, as an author, to get new readers involved. Thank you for spending the time with me, the team of authors in this series and the population of Trinity Lakes.

Meredith Resce

☺

ALSO IN THE TRINITY LAKES SERIES

Never Find Another You

Book#1 – Never Find Another You by Narelle Atkins

Hannah Gilbertson has deep roots in Trinity Lakes. Sporty and hard working, she loves running the rowing club and supporting the town's tourism. She's determined to avoid becoming entangled in her mother's matchmaking schemes, and wants to prove to her successful father she's worthy of carrying on his legacy.

Joel Manning left a broken heart behind in Australia to embark on a year long working vacation, and he's not looking for love.

The handsome Aussie captures Hannah's interest when she hires him to do work at her rowing club. Joel is drawn to the beautiful American, and a friendship develops.

A shocking secret combined with family upheaval leads to more questions than answers, and threatens to push Joel and Hannah apart. Can a growing love overcome the miles between them?

Now Available

I'll Always Choose You

Book#3 – I'll Always Choose You by Lisa Renee

Leah Thompson's father is Sheriff of Trinity Lakes. No one is good enough for his baby girl, and at twenty-four, she still has him vetting any potential relationships.

Justin has a past the sheriff won't forgive, but has loved Leah for years - the woman no guy has been brave enough to pursue. Who would want the grumpy sheriff as their future father-in-law? Except Justin is willing to do anything to win Leah's heart, even set her up on a fake date with his neck-tattooed mate from Australia. Surely the sheriff will see Justin is the better choice.

Available from April 2023

ALSO BY MEREDITH RESCE

Organized Backup

By Meredith Resce

Regency romance author, Luella Linley, arranges her characters' lives, making sure that they weather all storms and live happily-ever-after. Her characters are putty in her hands, but her 21st Century adult children are not so easily organized. When her daughter, Megan, asks for support with an inappropriate situation at work, Luella decides Megan should get a boyfriend to intimidate her boss. The cop who just pulled Luella over for speeding is a likely candidate.

Cam Fletcher is expecting to be interviewed by a famous author. Instead of sharing insights into his job working in the police force, he is sharing a meal with the famous author and her daughter, Megan. When left alone with Megan, Cam wonders when the interview will begin. The parents' extended absence gives him a clue, which Megan confirms. Luella Linley is playing matchmaker, but is he willing to play the game.

Book #2 in Luella Linley – License to Meddle series

In Want of a Wife

Can she hit the target twice in a row? Luella Linley can't resist the opportunity to show her daughter's picture to the handsome lawyer. What can it hurt? But Chloe is not amused at her mother's attempts to matchmake … except the man is a lawyer, and she has an unjust speeding ticket she wants to fight in court.

Book #3 in Luella Linley – License to Meddle series

All Arranged

by Meredith Resce

Luella Linley should feel satisfied that she has been instrumental in getting her two daughters happily settled. Her meddling was successful, but came at a price, and husband, Russell, has advised she leave the children to their own devices.

But her eldest, Pete, is thirty-five, living back at home and discouraged. His fiancée left him days before the planned wedding and six months on, Pete still hasn't recovered. Louise might be biased, but her responsible, hard-working and handsome son would make a good husband and father—but he's given up after three failed relationships. He is a good catch, but unlikely to be fooled by his mother's scheming and meddling as she did with his sisters.

This situation calls for something special. A direct approach. Just like in her novels. Let the parents do the arranging and sort out the wheat from the chaff. This method will take any risk of rejection out of the equation, and let's face it, a mother can tell what's needed for a successful long-term relationship.

Carrie Davis dedicated herself to her career long ago. Her one and only serious relationship was a disaster, put down mainly to her youthful naivety at the time. Up until the birth of her niece, Carrie had not considered that she might even like a relationship, but now thoughts of loneliness are stalking her. Carrie's sister, Ellen, knows and when she sees an odd advert in the classified ads, she begins to wonder if this is a prank or an opportunity sent from heaven. "Wanted. For a social experiment. A family arranged marriage."

ABOUT THE AUTHOR

South Australian Author, Meredith Resce, has been writing since 1991, and has had books in the Australian market since 1997.

Following the Australian success of her *Heart of Green Valley* series, they were released in the UK.

The Ocean Between Us is Meredith's 24th published title.

Apart from writing, Meredith teaches high school students. She is an avid reader, particularly Christian fiction. She is a fan of British costume-drama television series, and British cosy mystery shows. Jane Austen, L.M. Montgomery and Charles Dickens are favorite classic authors. Meredith is a country-girl at heart, and takes every opportunity to visit the farm where she grew-up.

Aussie rules football and cricket are her choice when following televised sport. Come on Aussies!

Meredith often speaks to groups on issues relevant to relationships and emotional and spiritual growth.

Meredith has also been co-writer and co-producer in the 2007 feature film production, *Twin Rivers* now available on Amazon Prime.

With her husband, Nick, Meredith has worked in Christian ministry since 1983.

Meredith and Nick have three adult children.

http://www.meredithresce.com

www.facebook.com/MeredithResceAuthor

Printed in Great Britain
by Amazon